LOVE TODAY MAXIM BILLER

Translated from the German by Anthea Bell

SIMON & SCHUSTER
New York   London   Toronto   Sydney

Simon & Schuster
1230 Avenue of the Americas
New York, NY 10020

Originally published in German in 2007 as *Liebe heute* by Verlag Kiepenheuer & Witsch.
Liebe heute by Maxim Biller

First Simon & Schuster hardcover edition June 2008

SIMON & SCHUSTER and colophon are registered trademarks of Simon & Schuster, Inc.

For information about special discounts for bulk purchases, please contact Simon & Schuster Special Sales at 1-800-456-6798 or business@simonandschuster.com.

Designed by Kate Susanna Moll

Manufactured in the United States of America

10 9 8 7 6 5 4 3 2 1

Library of Congress Cataloging-in-Publication Data

Biller, Maxim, date.
  [Liebe heute. English]
  Love today / Maxim Biller ; translated from the German by Anthea Bell. —
1st ed.
     p. cm.
  1. Love stories, German. I. Bell, Anthea. II. Title.
  PT2662.I448L5413 2007
  833'.914—dc22   2008011027

ISBN-13: 978-1-4165-7265-7
ISBN-10:   1-4165-7265-1

It was probably all in July, for the lime
trees were in flower.

—Boris Pasternak, *Safe Conduct*

The Mahogany Elephant

He waited for her for three months. He sorted out his photos, rearranged his books, moved some of the furniture around, and then he went on waiting. After that he read all the letters he had ever received and threw most of them away, and he bought a large map of India and hung it above his bed. Or rather he didn't buy a map of India, but that was what he really wanted to do while he was waiting. He waited and waited, and began to write a story about waiting for her, but he didn't know how it would end, so he dropped it. Finally he did nothing at all; he didn't even wait anymore. He was sleeping less and less, he ate nothing but bread and tomatoes and yellow supermarket cheese, and then at last she came back, they sat together on his sofa, and she said, "It's been a long time."

"Yes," he said, although he had firmly made up his mind to say as little as possible, "it's been a very long time."

She had lost weight on her travels, and he didn't think she looked better than before. She was tired, but then, she was always tired; she'd gone away to recover from feeling tired all the time, and now that she was back she was still tired. And she'd grown older. Older or more serious or harder, he wasn't sure which. There was a gray tinge to her suntanned skin, the kind you usually see only on older women, her smile was much too grave and thoughtful, and her cheekbones were even more prominent than before.

She rose to her feet and went out. When she came back she had a bright-colored bag in her hand.

"This is for you," she said.

"Thank you, my love," he said. He opened the bag. There was a small, fat, black mahogany elephant in it.

"Would you like a drink?" he asked.

"Some water."

"I bought wine for you."

"No, water," she said.

He slowly stood up and brushed his leg against hers. Apart from the fleeting kiss when she arrived it was their first physical contact in three months.

"Really just water?" he called from the kitchen, but she didn't reply. "Chilled or room temperature?" he asked, and she called quietly back, "Room temperature."

He took a new crate of water out of the closet, pushed it straight back in again with his foot, and opened the bottle of wine that had been standing on the kitchen table for the last six weeks. He picked up the glasses and the bottle, and before going back to the living room he took the elephant out of his trouser pocket and threw it in the garbage.

"Jordi," she said, "I didn't want wine."

"No," he agreed, "it's still too early for wine."

"I didn't drink at all while I was there," she said.

"That's a pity," he said.

"No, I don't think so."

"I think it is."

He poured wine first for himself, then for her, and they clinked glasses. She didn't look in his eyes, and she drank only a tiny sip before going into the kitchen to fetch a bottle of water. She sat down on the sofa again, as far from him as she had been just before, and began telling him about her travels—but he was barely listening. While she was away he had kept trying to imagine where she was at any given time, and what it was like there, but now he couldn't care less about India, he just wanted to know what her decision was. Of course, he knew already, but he wanted to hear it from her own mouth. He wanted her to suffer a little, he wanted her to have to say it and feel unhappy about hurting him. No, she would say, we're not going to get married, Jordi, I know that's not what I want now, so we'll never see each other again, the way we agreed.

"Did you miss me?" he said.

"No, Jordi," she said, "I didn't."

"Of course not," he said, and nodded.

"Are you angry?"

"No."

"I'm glad."

"Good."

"Are you sure you're not angry?"

"I'm sure."

He looked out the window. When she had left, you could still see right over the square to the Church of Zion. Now the trees were in leaf, and all you saw from the window were those wonderful large green leaves. The leaves swayed back and forth in the wind, reminding Jordi of seaweed drifting in the ocean.

Perhaps it was because they hadn't seen each other for so long. They hadn't seen each other for almost as long as they'd known each other! He laid his arm on the back of the sofa behind her and left it there for a few minutes, but then he took it away again. The arm didn't feel quite sure of itself.

"What about you?" she asked.

"Me?"

"What have you been doing?"

"Why didn't you call?" he said. "Not once in three months!"

"But you know," she said, taking alarm. "That was our agreement, wasn't it?"

She was right. She'd even said, "Suppose I stay there for good?" And he had said that would be okay, she was a free agent, and if they never said another word to each other again that would be okay too. But he had said so only out of calculation, because he knew that she was an Aries—and just try keeping a ram captive.

"There's a story about that elephant," she said. She paused, waiting for him to ask what the story was, but all he was thinking about was how to get the elephant out of the rubbish bin again without her noticing.

"It was the fourth," she said, "honestly, it was the fourth, I swear it."

He still didn't say anything. Then he went into the kitchen without a word, and before bending over the trash he turned around, to be on the safe side.

"I lost the first three!" she called from the living room. "Can you imagine it—all three of them? Do you think that means something?"

He was frantically searching through the garbage, but he couldn't find the elephant. He dug his hands deeper and deeper into the damp, smelly trash, and then he took everything out and laid it on the floor.

"I know this one's ugly!" she called again. "I bought it at the airport in Bombay. You should have seen the others. They were really pretty!"

He couldn't find it. He knelt, sweating, with the trash of the last three days spread out on the floor around him, and suddenly he realized how crazy he was. He thought, If she sees this she'll think I'm totally crazy, and he began picking up the trash and stuffing it back in the garbage can.

"Actually that's not true. I didn't want to bring you anything back." There she was behind him all of a sudden. "I simply forgot about you."

He turned his head and looked up at her from below. She ran her hand through his hair and said, "And then I remembered you again in Bombay, at the airport. . . . What's the matter? Have you thrown it away already?"

"Yes," he said.

"Then we're quits," she said. She knelt down beside him and helped to pick up the trash. It was soon done, and then they washed their hands together in the bathroom, looked at each other in the mirror, and smiled.

"Would you go out, please?" she said.

She had never felt shy about going to the bathroom in front of him before. Although he didn't really like it when she did, he would have given anything for her not to send him out now. He closed the door behind him and went into the living room. He sat down on the sofa, but got up again the next minute and put some music on. It was a CD they'd listened to together a couple of times, so he quickly turned it off. He sat down on the sofa again and looked out the window, watching the large green leaves swaying in the wind, and then he didn't feel so bad after all. It was as if he himself had just come back from a journey, a very good one, but difficult too; indeed, often simply tedious. And now he was back, glad not to be travelling, glad he could just sit here where he had sat for years, looking out the window at the large green leaves and enjoying them, and waiting for them to fall so that he could see the church behind them and be glad to think they would soon be growing again.

Before she went away, they'd tried it on the sofa once. No, he had tried it; she had gone along with him at first, but then she suddenly crossed her arms over her bare breasts. He ran his hand over her belly, and she pressed her legs firmly together. He turned away, disappointed, and she said it was horrible of him to punish her like that. After her flight had taken off, he sent her a text message apologizing, and perhaps she had seen it when the plane stopped over in Zurich, or perhaps not.

How much longer would she stay on the toilet? She usually took very little time about it—he was always surprised how little time she needed—but she went very often. He sometimes had to go frequently, too, but only when he was nervous, which maybe meant that she was always nervous. Today was different, this was the first time she'd gone to the bathroom since arriving, and she had been here for two hours. So today she wasn't as nervous as usual! As soon as that thought occurred to him he felt nervous and wanted to go to the bathroom himself.

He sat there for a while, waiting. Ten minutes must have passed, and then he couldn't wait any longer and went over to the bathroom. The door was closed, so he knocked, but there was no answer. He knocked again, louder, and now he heard her.

"I'm here," she said quietly.

"Where?"

"Here," she said even more quietly.

She was in the bedroom. She was lying in his bed fully clothed, and when he came in she said, "All right, let's get married." She lay there in his bed fully clothed, and then she turned on her side, she laid her head on the pillow and put her hands under it, and looked at him gravely and sadly.

Seven Attempts
at Loving

The first time, they were sitting side by side at school lunch in the kindergarten on Slavíkova Street, showing each other their little secrets under the table. She only had to open her legs slightly, he unbuttoned his trousers. It was always rather dark at the kindergarten, and they didn't see much. When they had had lunch all the children went into the big dormitory. Jirka followed Alena slowly and was sorry his bed wasn't next to hers. After that they played together, as he could still remember, although what they had played he didn't recollect. When their parents fetched them they did not say good-bye. They looked away, and the next day they didn't talk to each other. A few days later Alena pinched her own forearm until it was bright red. She yelled with pain, and when the kindergarten teacher was cuddling her Alena said, through her tears, that Jirka had done it.

Alena and Jirka were children of the Vinohrady district. It made no difference to them at the time, but later on they both often thought of that. He lived with his parents in Mánesova Street, up at the top by the square where the big rectangular church with the see-through clock stood. If the window in his room was open, he heard the trams going along Vinohradská Street. She lived in Chopinova Street. She only had to cross the road to reach the park. They often saw each other there, and just before his family and hers fled to the West in '68 he met her at the side of the park where you could look down at the city. It was late summer, the setting sun bathed the castle in lilac, and Alena was playing hopscotch with her girlfriends on the asphalt path. They'd drawn lines with blue and yellow chalk, they were hopping from square to square on one leg, and Alena didn't notice Jirka passing with his mother. Only when they reached the sports ground did he hear Alena call his name. He turned, and she ran toward him. When they were facing each other, she said, "We're going away soon, Jirka." He didn't reply, but his mother said quietly, "Alenka, I'm sure you're not supposed to tell anyone." He didn't yet know that his own parents were making similar plans, and he would soon see Alena again at the transit camp in Friedland.

"See you," he said, and for the first time in ages he took his mother's hand again and drew her away.

In Friedland, Alena and her parents were in the hut right beside the exit from the camp. Perhaps that gave them hope. They were still there when Jirka and his parents arrived that winter. It was a few days before he and Alena discovered each other. Alena had grown during the six months since they last met; she had small breasts now, and often wore the short, pale blue skirt that her mother had made her in Prague. Jirka didn't like Alena so much anymore. She was reading all the time, and when she wasn't reading her mind was elsewhere.

"What are you doing this afternoon, Alena?"

No reply.

"Shall we go to the cinema in town?"

"The cinema?"

"Yes."

"I don't know."

"Alena, it's no fun sitting around indoors the whole time."

"What did you say?"

"Oh, never mind."

A pause.

"Sure you wouldn't like to come with me, Alenka?"

Still no answer.

When Jirka and his parents moved to Frankfurt the next spring, Alena gave him one of her Czech books. The cover showed a young woman with long black hair framing her face, like a harp turned upside down. Her eyes were blue, her mouth was black. Jirka put the book on the bookshelf in his new room, and when he thought of Alena he took it out and looked at it. He took it out less and less as time went on. Sometimes he didn't look at it at all for two or three years, or he picked it up just by chance. As he remembered Alena, she looked like the young woman on the cover of the book, and when he went to study in Munich he took it with him.

Alena was planning to study in Munich too. Just before she went there her parents phoned his parents, and Jirka's mother said she was sure Alena could stay with Jirka when she went to register at the university.

Alena stayed there for three days. At first they hardly recognized each other, then they talked Czech, fast and excitedly, and suddenly they didn't feel so much alone. Jirka went to Adalbertstrasse with Alena when she registered, he showed her the canteen in the Art Academy, and the Venezia, and they slept in the same bed. On her last night he tried to kiss her. She was wearing a see-through nightie, and he put his hand on her breasts. They weren't as small as they had been in Friedland. She did not return his kiss, and pushed his hand away. In the morning she got up early and went back to her parents in Hamburg until the beginning of the semester. She didn't mention the kiss, but Jirka felt ashamed of himself. He wasn't in love with her, he thought, so why hadn't he left her alone? After the door had closed behind her it struck him that she really did look like the girl on the cover of the book.

At the last film festival in the Artists' House—this was a good deal later—they suddenly found themselves standing side by side. After that they were a couple. Before, they had seen each other about once a year, somewhere in the city, or in the little café in Amalienstrasse, and all they'd said was, "Hi, how are you?" In fact they were doing much the same thing now. They stayed together for four months, and it ended as it had begun—without many words. Alena went to collect Jirka from the School of Journalism, and they walked through the city to the river Isar. She held his hand, after a while she slowly let go of it, and he knew she would never hold hands with him again. Later, in his room, she sat at his desk under the large Face poster of the little boy with the gangster's hat, and she slowly turned the chair round in a circle. He took her to the U-Bahn station on Josephsplatz, and as they passed the tall old buildings in Isabellastrasse he thought of the tall old buildings of Vinohrady.

Three weeks after the revolution he was back in Prague to write a piece for *Die Weltwoche*, and when he returned to Munich he was dreaming of a Vinohrady apartment. He soon forgot the idea again, but after his next visit to Prague it was just the same—yet again he wanted to stay and yet again, after a week back in Munich, he didn't mind one way or the other about Prague. This went on for quite a while, and then his parents bought an apartment in Chopinova Street. After that, and when his parents were in Frankfurt, he went to Prague to work for a few months every year. Sometimes he stood outside their old apartment building in Mánesova Street and listened to the trams driving past on Vinohradská Street.

Since his first kiss Jirka had slept with eighteen women, he had kissed nine but done no more with them, he had gone almost all the way with three; he'd had three real girlfriends and an affair of some length which still kept flaring up again, and he had been with Alena for four months. Since *her* first kiss Alena had had three real boyfriends, one of them being Jirka, she had kissed someone five times, and she had once risked a one-night stand which was better than she had expected. Now she was married to a German architect twelve years her senior, she had no children, and she often thought of Jirka. When she went back to Prague again for the first time, in the spring of 2002, she was very excited. She hoped to meet him there by chance.

She did meet him in the city—outside Tesco. They were both waiting for the Number 22 tram, and for the first few minutes Alena didn't say a word. She just smiled and put the hair back from her face. Then the tram arrived, and they boarded it together. The tram drove off fast, then stopped abruptly, and all the passengers were thrown backward. Alena decided to make use of this opportunity. She fell into Jirka's arms, he held her tight and only slowly let her go. They both got out in Peace Square and went to their old park.

Jirka and Alena saw each other every day. They phoned each other in the morning and made a plan of some kind for the afternoon, and sometimes they stayed together for their evening meal. Alena too was based in Chopinova Street, in the building where she had grown up, staying with neighbors who had lived there for forty years. She was in Number 4 and Jirka was in Number 12, and they always split the difference fairly by meeting outside Number 8.

After a few days Jirka began giving up the morning phone calls. He often didn't call Alena back until the afternoon, saying he'd been overworked and he was afraid he was too tired to do anything now. Once they didn't see each other for three days, and he hoped Alena would stop calling entirely.

She didn't call, but she dropped in. She stood in the doorway before him, and in her white blouse and her short blue skirt she looked just like her mother and his own in the old days. She looked the way almost all Czech women looked in the sixties: stern, sexy, and older than she really was.

"I'm leaving tomorrow," said Alena, and suddenly it was all just the same as back then in the park when she was playing hopscotch with her girlfriends, and he had thought he'd never see her again.

"Come in," he said.

"Oh, no," she said.

"Please."

She came in and stood in the foyer. He asked if she'd like something to drink, and she drank a glass of water without sitting down.

"Do you have someone?" she said.

"No," he said.

"Oh, well," she said, "it doesn't really matter."

"No," he said.

"I'm never coming back to Prague again," she said.

"I can understand that," he said.

She began to cry, turned, and went away. He stood in the doorway and watched her going down the stairs, and then he stood on the balcony and looked after her as she left. She went slowly down Chopinova Street, and after every few steps she stopped, shed tears, and then went on again.

The Maserati
Years

It was a very cold day. He hadn't closed the balcony door over-night, and when he breathed out, a small cloud of vapor rose from his mouth. He lay in bed with only his face showing outside the covers, making clouds of vapor. Another five, no, another ten of them, and then he'd get up.

She hadn't kissed him when she awoke at dawn. She had reached for him, and when he was lying on top of her she didn't give him any help, but it was quite easy all the same. She didn't kiss him afterward either, and he went to sleep again straightaway and dreamed of a bottle of Corona as large as the water pump in Monbijouplatz.

Then he woke up once more, it was afternoon, and he thought of the big bottle of Corona. He'd have liked a cigarette, but he didn't have any left. He went to the bathroom, came back, turned his cell phone on, and put it down again. "Hi, Tom-Cat, I'm pregnant. Sorry to tell you this way. Going to my parents."

Two other text messages had arrived, both from someone at the production company, who had also left messages on his voice mail, sounding rather angrier every time, asking where he was. There'd been a rehearsal at one o'clock, someone would be there until six.

"Hi, Tom-Cat, I'm pregnant. Sorry to tell you this way. Going to my parents."

Oh, go to hell, he thought, breathing out another little cloud. Number four.

They were three friends meeting again after many years. One was now a singer, one was a doctor, and the third, the part he played, was nothing much. His character had never left home—he still lived with his family—and he wasn't as handsome as he used to be, but you could see that he once had been. During the single night depicted in the film, everything would change for all of them. *The Lost Night*. Not a bad title, if a little too American.

He still had the cooking sherry his mother had bought the last time she visited, and maybe there was a bottle of wine somewhere. A cigarette would be better. He imagined the smoke filling his lungs, slowly making him dizzy, and then the smoke would have to leave them again, although he'd prefer not to breathe it out at all. Little cloud number five.

I'll have to sell the car, he suddenly thought. He was surprised to find himself thinking that, but it was exactly what he thought. I'll have to sell the car, I can't afford it anymore if I have to pay up every month. Not this car, anyway. Step on the gas too hard and something goes off, *bang*, and the guy from Brunnenstrasse has to come and tow it away, and you take taxis until he's got hold of a new engine, and an engine like that costs a bundle. So there go the Maserati years, he thought, and for a moment he felt sad. Then he felt furious, and then he closed his eyes and went to sleep.

When he woke up it was getting dark again. Not entirely dark yet, but pretty dark. It was gray, blue-gray outside—the kind of light you got only at the end of November, the beginning of December, at around three or three-thirty in the afternoon, when Berlin might as well be in Finland.

Three or three-thirty—right. He got up, went to the bathroom, and on the way back he looked in the big kitchen drawer to see if there were any cigarettes there. He didn't find any, and he picked up the sherry bottle, but then he put it down again. Once back in bed he felt for a moment the way he used to as a child, walking around the apartment on a Sunday while the others were still asleep. Since there was no one who wanted to play with him he would go back to bed, and the bedclothes were as perfectly cool as they felt now.

They had never discussed it. He hadn't asked her any questions, and she hadn't said anything. He thought, If she doesn't say anything then there's nothing to discuss, nothing can happen. It was that way with other women. If there'd been anything to discuss she would surely have said something, he'd thought, and now he was thinking that of course that had been stupid of him. She would have said something only if she didn't want any problems. So either there was nothing to discuss, or she did want problems.

When he first met her, in the Casolare, he'd thought, This is going nowhere, and if it does go anywhere then it won't be for long. He had looked out at the canal and ordered successive glasses of wine for her, thinking the same thing all the time. Presumably, she had been thinking something quite different. She had black hair, blue eyes, and a look that could bring you to tears. He thought, That's how it is when they're a little older, they're often like that. They aren't ashamed of anything in bed, though, and you don't have to feel ashamed of anything with them either.

His mobile rang, and he jumped up at once. When he saw that it was someone from the production company he let it ring. It stopped, and then a text came in from the wardrobe supervisor, but he deleted it without reading it and went back to bed. Then he got up again and closed the balcony door.

He put some music on, lay down, and listened to Al Green, and thought how he'd never listen to Al Green in his beautiful car anymore. It was still rather cold in the room, he'd pulled the quilt right up to his chin, and the cold wind was like the wind that blew in his face in the Maserati. He drove up Leipziger Strasse to Potsdamer Platz and then on west. He listened to "La-La for You," and the white winter sun danced between the buildings ahead of him.

The Biturbo really was a beautiful car. Its engine had a pleasant, stern sound, it sat five people, and it was as angular as a chocolate box. And now all that was over because she hadn't told him he had to take care. They'd done it ten or perhaps twelve times, even when she'd had her period. They'd been good together, he'd enjoyed himself and so had she, and now he'd have to get rid of his beautiful car.

He breathed out through his mouth, but nothing happened. He tried again, but the air in the room wasn't cold enough anymore. He could feel the warmth of the radiator behind the bed. You could almost touch that warmth, and when he thought of the cold weather outside he didn't want to go out at all.

They wouldn't be shooting without him anyway. They couldn't go on shooting without him! Niklas had written the part specially for him—his character in the film was a little like his real self. Niklas had often said so, and he hadn't always liked that, but mostly it was okay. Now he was glad, because they really couldn't do without him, even in rehearsal.

Anyway, at the moment everyone wanted to make films featuring him.

Or no, of course they could manage without him. And who in fact did still want to make films featuring him? Exactly—people who hadn't worked with him before. He was always offered the same kind of part, and that was his own doing—he could have said no. The directors he'd started out with worked with other people now, just throwing him the occasional bone out of charity. A small part in the film, large letters in the opening credits: "Guest appearance by our old friend Feri, and no, we don't know why we're doing this either."

Shit, I want to make more little clouds, he thought. He got up, opened the balcony door, and crawled back into bed. It was dark in the room, but he didn't switch a light on. It wasn't gray or blue-gray outside the window anymore, it was dark, almost black. From outside, a little of the ugly orange East Berlin street lighting filtered in, and the objects in the room seemed to quiver slightly in it. His breath immediately turned to vapor outside his mouth, and he felt as if the air in his lungs were lost forever.

Number seven, he thought. Then he made the other three and closed his eyes. He fell asleep, woke up ten minutes later, and went into the kitchen. He drank his mother's sherry, went to the bathroom, lay down, and dropped off to sleep again. He slept half the night, and then there was a text message.

"Hi, had a fright? Just wanted to see how cold you really are. Don't ever call me again. Miaow."

He switched off his phone, went into the bathroom, and showered. He took a very long, very hot shower, and he kept thinking: Go to hell. Then he lay down and tried to sleep, and it worked better than he'd expected.

The Statement
by Amos Oz

They sat down on a bench in Innocentia Park, and Bella said, "Do people always know what they're writing?"

At the same time Amos Oz, Amos Kollek, David Grossmann, and a couple of others were on their way through the evening streets of Jerusalem to visit the prime minister and hand him the statement they'd been working on all day. They were tired and nervous, and as they travelled in three cars they called one another a few times during the drive, for encouragement and to wish one another luck. When they reached the prime minister's

residence near the Jaffa Gate they got out and stood around
the cars for a while, talking quietly. Then they went in.

Dusk was slowly falling now in Innocentia Park. He was
beginning to feel cold, but he didn't say anything. Bella had
been cold for quite a long time, and she said she was hungry.
They went down the path on the Isestrasse side of the park
one last time, and he wanted to put his arms around her or at
least place his hand on her back. He could easily have done
it, because at that very moment she was wondering what it
would be like to rest her chin on his shoulder and look past
him and up at the evening sky. So as they walked along she
let her shoulder brush his arm, as if by chance, but he didn't
react. After, both of them looked, at the same time, at the
great expanse of grass slowly disappearing into the darkness,
while the streetlamps came on one by one, and the grassy
space lay silver as a lake in the middle of the park.

The Café de Paris was empty. A few people were sitting
outside in a Sunday frame of mind, looking tired and con-
tent, and you could see that their thoughts were already on
the new working day tomorrow. As usual, the light in the café
was too dim. It was even dimmer and dingier at the back,
where they sat down.

They sat side by side on the banquette in silence for a
while, then they looked at the menu, and Bella said she'd like
the schnitzel and got to her feet. When she came back he felt
for a moment as if he hadn't seen her for weeks, and now she
was back again at last. She felt the same when she saw him,

but hers was a slightly different feeling. She often had different kinds of feelings. At New Year's in the synagogue where they suddenly found themselves talking to each other she'd had a very good feeling; not so good when he went back to Frankfurt; better when he came back. Just now it was getting worse again.

She sat down beside him, but a little farther away than before. "Do we have to talk about it?" she said.

"No," he said, "we don't have to."

"You want to, though."

"That's not me," he said, smiling, "it's my impatience."

"I want to go slowly," she said. "This time I must take it very slowly."

"I know."

"I know you know."

"We know all about it anyway," he said.

"Yes, we know all about it," she said. "That's good, but it's also . . ." She hesitated.

"Dangerous?" he said.

"Yes, dangerous," she said. "But let's not say so anymore. 'Dangerous' isn't the right word."

She took his hand, and he tried to kiss her on the neck. She leaned toward him but turned away at the same time, and then the waiter brought their order.

The statement drawn up for the prime minister by Amos Oz, Amos Kollek, David Grossmann, and the rest was not just a statement like any other. They themselves didn't know how it had come into being, and when they had finished it was too late to change anything. The text was somber, full of long words, and not particularly specific. It spoke of the downfall of Israel, of the prophets and the children of Ishmael, and the blood-red evening sun above the Negev was mentioned three times. While they sat in his living room drinking tea, the prime minister had taken the statement into his study. When he came back he looked very frightened, but perhaps he was just angry with them. Then his son came out of a back room shouting that one of those bastards had blown himself up in Petach Tikva—the Security Cabinet would have to meet tonight. The prime minister nodded and said very well, but first he wanted to talk to these writers. Then he sat down in the living room with them, and they began to talk, and he kept asking them why they were so certain of their case.

"And why are *you* so certain of yours?" they said.

"I just am," he said.

"But that's nonsense."

"No. It would be nonsense to be able to explain it."

Bella and he crossed the Rathausplatz, and the city was very dark here; when they looked up at the buildings almost all the windows were black. Then they went down to the river Alster, past the Vier Jahreszeiten hotel, and on the Kennedy Bridge they turned around for a moment. The Jungfernstieg shone white and cool in the night. There were hardly any cars around, and the Christmas lights blinked from the Neuer Wall.

"Paris," he said.

"Too romantic," she said.

"London."

"It's always so drafty there."

"New York."

"Don't want to," she said.

"Budapest. How about Budapest?"

"Are you crazy?"

"Budapest makes people feel happy."

"In winter?"

"Well, perhaps not in winter."

"Maybe I'll come and see you in Frankfurt over the holiday," she said, and she felt good when she said that. She waited to see if a different feeling would come, but it didn't. And then it did after all, but she more or less succeeded in ignoring it.

"Maybe yes or maybe no?" he said.

She took his hand in silence, and put it in her jacket pocket along with her own hand. It took him a moment to match his walking pace to hers, and he noticed for the first time that she strode as firmly and purposefully as a man. They went down Grindelallee in silence, and when they passed the big black hole where the Bornplatz Synagogue used to stand they said nothing, although they were both thinking the same thing. Then they each thought separately that this thought was awkward for them, and then they thought of nothing anymore, because they were very tired by now.

Before they disappeared into the night, Bella said, "Why do you think anyone wants to conquer someone else?"

"I don't know."

"Really not?"

"Maybe to discover that person's secret."

"And then what?"

"Then it's been discovered."

"Or not."

"Well, then you have to conquer that person again."

"Again and again," she said, "every day, every night."

She stopped and put her arms around him, and then they went on.

"Are you going to write a story about us?" she said.

"You first," he said.

"You idiot," she said, laughing, and suddenly a big black cloud came in front of the moon, the street lighting flickered and went out all over Hallerplatz.

That night the prime minister had less than two hours of sleep. When it was all over, and he was finally in bed, all kinds of ideas kept racing through his mind. He had already taken some tablets, and when they didn't help, Dr. Zwetnoy came and gave him an injection. After a while his pulse slowed, his heart beat regularly, and that terrible sense of pressure left his head. What a night! Fifteen dead, countless injured; that fool from General Staff who'd been slowing him down for weeks; his fervent desire to kill all those bastards wherever they might be found; the writers and their strange statement. He switched off his bedside lamp and looked out the window. The orange light on the façade of the building opposite flickered and faded. Day was beginning to dawn over Jerusalem, but at last he finally closed his eyes and tried to forget this night. He was afraid, terribly afraid—for he knew that everything Oz, Kollek, and the others had said in their statement would come true one day.

The Architect

When they woke up in the morning the architect was already sitting at his computer. His office was in the right wing of the building; they lived in the left wing. The light was on all night in the inner courtyard. It would soon go off, and then at some point the architect would put the light out in his office too. Now, in winter, that might not be until midday. On particularly dark days he kept the light on until evening—until he finished work, leaving the office after everyone else, and took the elevator up to join his family.

He waved to them and immersed himself in his work again. He never made them feel that he was watching them, but nor did he think of drawing the drapes in his office. They didn't draw theirs either. Usually they just pushed one of those large aluminum blinds resembling aircraft wings from one side of the long window to the other. Sometimes they forgot to do it, woke up in the morning, and they could see him at work from their bed. Once they had sex on the sofa in front of the TV set in the middle of the day. He couldn't have failed to notice. But he never once raised his head, and to make phone calls he went back into the large room where his staff sat at long white tables, looking at their computer monitors all day long.

While Naila was in the bathroom, Splash made breakfast. They were in a hurry. They were almost never in a hurry, but Naila had to be in Jakobstrasse by ten, because her permit to stay ran out today, and he had a date to meet the one-eyed Icelander in Kopenhagener Strasse to show him the studio. He hated the idea of not being able to work alone in his studio anymore—but they needed the money. Anyway he was hardly ever there, so it made no difference. He hadn't done any work for almost a year, not since they started living together, and sometimes Splash thought that was to do with Naila. Then he thought it was to do with this building. It was far too transparent, glass and aluminum and black stone everywhere, and the trams rattled down Rosenthaler Strasse every few minutes, scaring away the few ideas he still had with the noise they made.

Naila came out of the shower naked. She had wrapped her hair in a towel, and when Splash nodded toward the architect she said, "He doesn't look anyway." Splash shrugged and went into the bathroom. When he had finished Naila was standing by the window in panties and his new blue T-shirt. The architect was standing at his window too, and they were both making funny gestures. Splash turned, went back into the bathroom, and came out again two minutes later. Naila was fully dressed, the architect was back at his desk.

The architect had designed this building himself. It was his first; that was why he found it so hard to part with it. Either he sat down there in his office, or he was up with his family. He left the building only in his car. He drove out of the garage, and when he came back he drove straight into the garage again, as if the car itself were a part of the building, and that way he never had to leave the place.

Splash usually met the architect's wife and children in the elevator or the entrance hall, which had walls clad with large, matt steel panels. It was so tall and narrow that you felt as if you were inside a rocket there. The architect's wife smiled a lot. She was small, almost as small as her children, and the children laughed a lot too, but Splash didn't believe their laughter was real. He had never mistrusted a child's laughter before. Probably he was being unjust, but he didn't believe the laughter of these children was real, because their mother's certainly wasn't. Or perhaps it was simply that the children didn't fit into these surroundings, in their brightly colored, ugly winter anoraks, the kind that every child wore, and their thick winter boots, which were usually smeared with mud.

"Are you going to the studio today, my darling?" Naila asked.

"My darling," said Splash impatiently. He used to be called Jörn, not Splash, but so far she had never called him by his real name.

"Well, are you going?"

"Yes."

"Oh, that's wonderful!" she said.

He looked at her and didn't know whether her delight was genuine. Sometimes Naila spoke in a tone of voice that he couldn't interpret. No doubt her friends and relations at home understood that tone of voice—but he didn't. He was angry, then he put his hand over Naila's, which was lying on the table almost as if it didn't belong to her, and he thought he could draw that hand sometime. It was a warm hand; he stroked it, turned it over, and opened it, and it was cold inside. So he put the palm of his hand on hers, and suddenly he stood up, leaned toward Naila, and kissed her. She didn't kiss him back. It had often been like that recently. When he tried to touch her breasts she retreated and said, "Stop it, he can see us!"

"I thought you said he didn't look."

"I did, I did," she said, and there it was again, that tone of voice he couldn't interpret. "I did," she repeated, and they both looked at the architect.

The architect was standing with his back to them, speaking on the phone. Plans hung on the wall behind his desk, and he looked at the plans as he phoned, but he kept turning his head to look at the two of them. He had never done that before, and after a while Splash had had enough of it. He took Naila's face firmly in both his hands and kissed her on the lips, in spite of her resistance. She pushed him away and ran into the bathroom, and when Splash looked up his eyes met the eyes of the architect. The sense of nausea in his stomach disappeared as quickly as it had come.

"Naila!" called Splash. "Quick, come here! You have to see this! I think he's gone crazy!"

The architect had been calmly continuing his phone conversation, but suddenly he threw the telephone on the floor, tore his plans off the wall, and swept his papers, the computer, and his models of buildings off the desk. His employees came in, two of them took him by the shoulders and tried to hold him and calm him down, but he broke free, ran to the window, and drummed his fists on it. In the end he slid down past the windowpane and fell exhausted to the floor, and his thin face with its large green eyes and the shock of untidy black hair over them looked more attractive than usual.

"That's what I'll do if they don't make long my permit to stay today," said Naila. She was standing behind Splash and had hooked her fingers into the belt loops of his jeans.

"If they don't *extend* my permit to stay today," he corrected her, and thought, Well, why not? Then he could start working again, and it wouldn't be all Naila, Naila, Naila anymore. Then he wouldn't have to keep talking to her about her life, then it would be none of his business that her mother had had an affair with her grandfather, that her father called her Puppi and often called her at night from Beirut, in tears, that Lebanese men were all idiots and that was why she liked the men here so much—too much, he thought—and he wouldn't have to continue living in this stupid, expensive, icy rocket of a building because of her anymore. He could move back into the studio in Kopenhagener Strasse, and he could tell the one-eyed Icelander today to look for some other place, he didn't need his money anymore, not ever.

"Do you know what's wrong with him?" said Naila.

"I thought you did," said Splash.

"Me? Why me?"

She put on her tall brown boots and the red Alaïa jacket that he hated so much—it was a present from her father—and said, "Do you have my keys?"

"Why are you always asking me for your keys? I never had your keys."

"But you can always find them."

"Not today."

"Please."

"No."

"Darling . . . my sunlight, my heart!"

He stood up and began clearing the table. He went back and forth between the table and the kitchen at least twenty times, always carrying just one plate, or one spoon, or just the damn butter dish. When the table was empty he sat down, lit a cigarette, and tried to concentrate. Should he call the Icelander and put off their meeting until the evening? By then he'd know whether Naila could stay on or not. Or should he call off the deal entirely? He'd already put the Icelander off twice, perhaps that meant he wouldn't turn up anyway. But maybe he wouldn't have to put him off at all. Yes or no? At that moment he heard the loud screech of a tram very close, and he jumped. An icy gust of wind touched his legs, the next tram thundered by, he looked up and saw that Naila had opened one of the huge windows.

"La-lala-lala," she went. She was strolling up and down the enormous room as if it were a park, she walked in a circle swaying her large Arab behind around. "La-lala-lala."

"Do shut that window, Naila," he said. "I can't think with all this noise."

"La-lala-lala."

"Naila, please."

"Only if you'll help me look for my keys."

He stood up, went to the coat stand, and took the keys out of the little inside pocket of her black leather jacket.

"How did you know they were there?"

"They always are," he said. "If they're not in another jacket. Or in the soap dish in the bathroom. Or in the drawer with the cookies. Or in the bed. Or under the mattress. Or under the bed."

"Thank you, my darling," she said, hugging him tentatively.

"My darling," he said.

"What will I do without you?" she said, smiling. There were tears in her eyes, and she kissed him on the cheeks and the mouth. Then she looked at him again, and the tears were gone. Had they ever been there at all? he wondered. Or was it just another act in her great big emotional Lebanese show?

"Don't worry," he said. "You'll get your papers today."

"Suppose I don't."

"Suppose you don't?"

"Yes—suppose I don't. Suppose I have to go home."

He looked at her gravely, she looked back at him gravely, and because he couldn't hold her gaze he looked past her at the room. It was not with his own eyes that he saw all this, it was with the eyes of someone he was not yet but soon might be. After he had seen it all, the bed, the two white Pierre Paulin armchairs, the silver lamp on its marble stand, the photos of Naila's family in gold frames on the TV set, and his old pictures on the high walls, after he had glanced briefly at the architect's dark and empty office, he looked into Naila's brown, very brown eyes again and said, "If you have to go back, my angel, then I'll go with you, of course."

"Would you do that?" she said, surprised. "Would you really do that . . . ?" She pushed his arms away and removed herself from his embrace. "Come on, I must go," she said. She pressed her thin, freshly painted lips together two or three times, and as she turned away she cast a last, surreptitious look at the other side of the inner courtyard.

They stood side by side in silence outside the elevator. They stood so that their arms and shoulders did not quite touch, and that was almost exciting once again. The elevator came, the door opened, and there stood the architect with his wife. Their children were all there too. Splash and Naila got in with them, they said hello, the architect said hello too, his wife smiled, and the children looked up and smiled as well.

The architect looked normal again. Splash watched him out of the corner of his eye as he stared past the heads of the architect and Naila to look at the gleaming silver wall of the elevator. He looked at Naila too now and then, and she seemed quite normal. Perhaps a little nervous, but that was natural. He would have been just as nervous in her position. He was nervous even when he had to go to the doctor, or get a visa from some consulate when he went on a journey. She had put off visiting the aliens' registration office until the very last day, out of anxiety, and he would have done just the same. So now she was nervous. Splash went on staring at the elevator wall, but all the same he noticed Naila and the architect briefly touching hands. She stroked the back of his own hand with her fingers, he clenched his fist, and after that she removed her hand again.

The elevator stopped on the first floor, and Splash and Naila got out. The architect and his family went on down to the garage. They said good-bye, and the elevator door closed behind them. Splash took Naila's hand, and they went out. They walked hand in hand to the tram stop, and when Naila boarded her tram and it drove off Splash watched her go. He even thought of waving, but then he didn't. He turned and walked down Rosenthaler Strasse to the suburban train station, and because the pedestrian lights outside the Hackesche Höfe took forever to come on he looked up at the rocketlike building. The matte, blue-gray glass façade looked dead in the hazy winter light. On two floors, lights were on at the front of the building—in the architect's place and in the publishing firm on the floor above—and in that greenish yellow neon lighting the people in the offices looked as if they were slowly drowning. Splash shook his head and swore quietly. Then he didn't feel like waiting in the crowd at the lights anymore, but what could he do? He waited all the same, until they turned green. Then they turned red again at once, then green again, then red again, and he still stood there, not knowing what to do.

My Name Was Singer

Usually I forget that I'm living at the wrong time and in the wrong place. In my last life I was a miracle-working eighteenth-century Polish rabbi, which was better. Now I'm a modern Jewish writer who writes in German. Of course I'd rather it were English or Hebrew.

The other day I was sitting in the Kastanienallee café where I'm a regular, and a woman began talking to me. She was very serious, but you could see she hadn't always been. She said she had read everything I'd written, she knew whole paragraphs from my stories by heart.

"You helped me to understand myself," she said. "You write about love in a way that a German writer never could. You're right, we Jews ought not to look for happiness with non-Jews."

When she said that I fell in love with her right away. I live in Mauerpark, not far from the café, and I asked if she'd like to come back to my place. But when we were lying in my bed she had problems. She preferred to talk. She told me about her German husband, and how she had written him a letter two years ago. Her letter said that she'd like to go back to her maiden name, which she had changed when she married. To this day her husband hadn't commented on her letter. And he hadn't written back either.

I tried to kiss her, but she turned her head away.

"What was your name before?" I asked.

"Norma Glickstein. Now my surname is Bressensdorf."

She began crying, and I tried to kiss her again. Once she had calmed down I said I was afraid I had some work to do, so she couldn't stay.

Another woman rang my doorbell last summer, at eleven at night. I have a video monitor showing the door to my building, and when I saw a nervous black-haired woman who was a stranger to me on the monitor I opened the door at once. She came upstairs quickly, and at my front door she said, "Please forgive me for taking you by surprise. I was in the area, and I felt: he'll let me in today. If you only knew how often I've stood outside your building before!"

A cold shudder ran down my back. A few times in my life I've met women with whom I felt a telepathic link, but I knew them and loved them already. I didn't want that kind of thing with a stranger.

"I know all about you from your books," she said. "But in spite of that you're still a riddle to me."

"Have you come here to solve it?" I asked. I imagined myself standing under the chuppa with this woman, making her pregnant right away, the two of us walking hand in hand along the beach of Tel Aviv in our old age.

"I used to be a crazy, drug-addicted Jewish girl in Berlin," she said. "Bobbed hair, twenty years old. I was burnt to death at Birkenau. Aren't you going to ask me in?"

"Please don't be cross, but I'm not feeling well, and I'm leaving for a conference in Antwerp first thing in the morning. Look in next week if you feel like it."

Luckily I never saw her again.

Why am I telling you all this? Because of Geli Schmelzer. Geli is the daughter of Leszek Schmelzer, a Polish Jewish writer who was very popular in Munich in the seventies and eighties. Geli and I had known each other as children. Two years ago, after a long gap, I was going back to Munich to give a reading in the cold, bleak municipal hall in Reichenbachstrasse. Afterward she came up to me and said, "Don't you remember me?"

"No," I said.

"I was the girl under the table."

"And I was the boy," I said, laughing, and kissed her on both cheeks.

"Were you always so beautiful?" I asked.

"Oh, yes," she said. "Of course."

Geli and I often used to sit under the white tablecloths on the big tables in our parents' apartments when their living rooms were full of guests. Most of the grown-ups didn't know we were hiding there. Some did know, but they didn't mind. There were often arguments, particularly about Israel, and now and then one of the women would shout at her husband, whereupon the husband, feeling insulted, would leave the room. But usually they all got on very well. Polish, Yiddish, and Russian were spoken, and of course German and English too. When Geli and I didn't want to listen to the grown-ups we traced numbers and letters on each other's backs with our fingers.

One of the guests was a thin man with red hair and a sly smile. He spoke English with a Polish accent, and a beautiful, clear Yiddish that Geli and I understood better than the Yiddish spoken by the ordinary Jews of Munich. He was a writer from New York. His wife came from Munich, and he travelled with her when she visited her family in the fall for the religious festivals. Once, late at night, we heard him telling a woman who wasn't his wife that he loved her. Then we saw him pressing his legs against hers. The two of them and we children were the only people in the room. There was a moment's silence, and suddenly he bent down to look under the table and said, "Don't you dare say a word to anyone, you little toads!" After that he pressed his legs against the woman's legs again, and she giggled and said she did a bit of writing herself.

I was glad to see Geli again after so many years. It was a long time since I'd had a woman in my life, and I liked Geli. She was small and slim, she looked like Ellen Barkin but not so sad, and I knew at once that she enjoyed sex. She asked if I was married or had a girlfriend. Instead of answering, I asked how about her.

"I'm just splitting up from someone," she said, "although unfortunately he's not splitting up from me."

We were standing outside on the corner of Reichenbach-strasse and Gärtnerplatz, and Geli said, "Come back to my place. I read your latest book. I'd like to talk to you about it."

"No," I said, "let's not do that. But take me home with you all the same."

The book was lying beside Geli's bed. It was a love story about a woman who can't do it although she wants to, and a man who wants to do it although the woman can't. After we were dressed again, Geli said, "There's just one thing I want to know: was it all exactly the same in real life as in your book?" I shook my head, and then she told me about Tuvia Katz, the man who wouldn't let her go. Tuvia wouldn't let her go, and his parents wouldn't let her go, and her own parents said, "Do as you like, darling, but you're not as young as you used to be."

I stayed a week longer than I'd meant to in Munich. As

soon as I was back in Berlin I called Geli and said, "We could get married if you like."

"Yes," she said, without hesitating. "But give me time. I don't want to hurt Tuvia."

I put the phone down and cursed. I knew that book.

Geli and I didn't see each other for over three months. After those three months there she suddenly was in front of me in Kastanienallee. I was in Café Napoljonska, thinking of her, and when I saw her I said, "I knew you were in Berlin."

"Yes," she said, "I know. And I'm sure you know the rest of it too."

"You haven't managed to make the break yet. You want to. Sometimes you love him, sometimes me. It's the most difficult time in your life. I'm the only person who could help you. But then I'm involved myself."

"Yes, you're right."

We went to my place, and in bed I traced, "I love you," with my finger on her bare back. She wrote something on my back that I couldn't make out. Then I wrote, "Leave him," on her back, and she wrote, "I'll try." Then she stayed another two days, and when she left we took a photograph of ourselves on my balcony. It's an amusing photo. I look like my father, she looks like her mother—but not when they were young.

A month later I called Geli and said, "You wanted me to phone."

"Yes."

"So?"

"You know."

"I don't understand."

"Yes, you do—you understand."

"What do I understand?"

She started crying. "I'm working for Tuvia now. In his office."

"You? As a secretary?"

"I have projects of my own as well. He needs me. He's had to fire almost all his staff. The real estate business is very bad at the moment."

"You don't want to live with me," I said.

"I'm writing stories myself now, André."

"Then read them aloud to him," I said furiously. "But maybe your prince of the ghetto can actually read himself."

She ended the call.

After that Geli and I spoke to each other only in our thoughts. I told her what a miracle it was that we had met. She said she knew. I asked: Why do you hesitate? Perhaps, she replied, because I don't love you. You do, I said. How do you know? she asked. I've never loved a woman who didn't love me, I said. And what about that woman in your last novel? she said. You're getting on my nerves, I said. I haven't heard from Geli since.

Recently I've been rereading Isaac Bashevis Singer. That helps me. I'm not interested in his historical novels; the shtetl, the Hasidim, and the dybbuks are not my world, although maybe I was a zaddik myself once. I like Singer's stories. They are about him and his women, and how he and they drive one another crazy. Human beings are always doing the wrong thing, says Singer, and it doesn't trouble him. He finds it interesting.

Of course that New York writer who scared Geli and me back then in the parental living room had been Singer. I realized it was Singer only very much later. When I first went to the Frankfurt Book Fair I met him again. He was sitting at the publisher Hanser's stand with Geli's father, and I said hello to them both. My first book was just out, and Leszek Schmelzer told Singer I was one of the great hopes of Jewish literature. My girlfriend was beside me, a tall, melancholy German girl who loved me very much. Singer asked her in German where she came from, how she was, and whether she liked my stories. "I love them," she said. Later, when she wasn't listening, he told me in Yiddish, "You want to beware of women who love your books." And as he said that, his nose was sharper and his smile slyer than usual.

Baghdad at Seven-Thirty

They were the first customers that day. It was just after five, and the man and the young woman came in without a word and sat down at the bar. He ordered a beer, she asked for a tea, and as they didn't serve tea she had a grapefruit juice. He drank his beer quickly, ordered another from the small black-haired waiter, then looked up at the TV monitor hanging over the bar. The sound was muted, and after a while he'd seen enough even without sound, and he turned to her.

The young woman sat there quite still, looking at Maximilianstrasse through the door, which was wide open. In spite of the heat she was wearing a trench coat. Under it she had a close-fitting black top and a gray pencil skirt, her legs were long and beautiful, and perhaps that was why she kept them pressed together the whole time. The young woman had the pale, precociously mature face of a ballet dancer, although she wasn't a dancer, but the way she sat there, bolt upright and proud, anyone would certainly have taken her for one.

He waited to see if she would look at him, but she didn't. He knew the small black-haired waiter was watching them, certainly thinking that he was too old and too stout for her. He ordered another beer and looked at the TV screen again.

"How can you keep on watching that?" she asked wearily.

"I don't know," he said. "You look at it, you look away, and when you look again you're just hoping it will all be over at last."

He was thinking of his son Frederic, and she too was thinking of his son Frederic, who was almost as old as she was, but neither of them said anything, because they had another problem just now. Perhaps Frederic was still in the States—his unit wasn't due to leave for Kuwait until next week—and perhaps by then it really would be over and he could stay at home after all. He thought, I ought not to have left him with Marcia when we split up, then he'd be a German today and not an American. She thought, I ought not to have started taking those damn pills, it's only because of him I'm taking them, and now I want to stop killing myself day by day, but I still don't want to live anymore.

"And sometimes it's interesting," he said. "You see the same tank driving through the desert twice, once from left to right, once from right to left. The same pictures, only back to front."

"Depends on the channel," said the small black-haired waiter.

"Yes," he said, "it depends on the channel."

"On CNN they always drive from right to left," said the waiter. "Going west."

"That's right," he said, "towards Baghdad."

"And here we always see them driving east."

"Well, almost always."

"Another beer?"

He leaned over to her and asked, "Would you like something else?"

She shook her head, almost imperceptibly.

"Yes, I'll have another beer," he told the waiter. "And then I'd like to be left to have a conversation in peace."

The waiter drew the beer without any change of expression and put it in front of him. A few drops landed on the shiny black bar counter, and the waiter wiped them off with a dish towel. Then he began polishing glasses, with his back turned to them.

"That was mean of you," she said.

"I apologize," he said. "I'll ask him his opinion, shall I? Maybe he knows how we can get out of this mess."

"I could stop taking the pills again," she said.

"I couldn't stand that. I can't stand you when you're so sad."

"But you can't stand me when I don't want to sleep with you either."

"Perhaps there are pills of some kind for that too," he said.

He caressed her cheek, and she went on looking past him and through the open doorway at Maximilianstrasse. He stroked a few strands of hair off her face and tucked them behind her large and beautiful ears, but she still didn't look at him. A pleasant breath of wind blew into the bar.

"You know I love you," he said.

"How much do you love me, then?"

"A lot. I really do."

"Do you love me more than yourself?"

"I think so."

"Then you ought not to mind."

"I do."

"Why?"

"Because it makes me unhappy. And it makes you unhappy."

"I don't mind whether we have sex or not," she said. "I mean, that's the problem."

"Maybe it isn't because of the pills at all."

"You know it is. The doctor said all medicinal drugs have side effects, and that's the side effect of this one. A medicinal drug without side effects, he says, is like a war without a loser."

"He said that?"

"Yes."

"Odd kind of doctor, don't you think?"

"Find me a better one."

"We already have the better one."

She smiled and looked briefly at him, then turned her gaze to the door again. The sunlight fell into the dark bar on a slant, like a curtain of a thousand little glass beads, and beyond it other customers were sitting at small white plastic tables on the terrace. Beyond them she saw the cars and trams driving down Maximilianstrasse, all of it as if through mist, and she wondered if that was because of the curtain of sunlight or her pills.

"Well, how's it going?" he asked, and turned to the bar.

The small black-haired waiter was still standing with his back to them, polishing glasses with the checked dish towel, and he looked up at the TV screen. "Oh, it's still a draw," he said, without moving.

"First or second half?"

"I'd say we're at the start of the second half. The American manager really lost his cool at halftime. They're putting on the pressure again."

"How about the Iraqis?"

"Retreated to their penalty area. It's going to be a tough game for the Yanks."

An abandoned Iraqi position came into sight on the screen. There were wrecked buildings and tired, unshaven Arab men searching the sandy ground for mines with their bare hands. Then came crying children in hospital beds much too large for them. Then Baghdad in the evening, in a venomous green light. Then soldiers, American prisoners. One of them was Frederic.

Or no, he wasn't. But he looked very much like Frederic.

"As long as they show them, we know they're all right," said the waiter.

"Yes," he said.

"Was that Frederic just now?" she said. She was leaning against him, and looked up at the screen with the two of them.

"No," he said, "thank God."

"I almost thought so," she said wearily. She patted his hands. He was holding tight to the dark, gleaming counter, and when he let go of it the counter was wet with his sweat.

What's all this playacting? he was thinking. She was always jealous of Frederic. She was thinking: Now it's really over, he doesn't believe me anymore.

"Another beer and then the check," he said. He pushed his empty glass across the counter and took the new one from the waiter. It was clouded with condensation on the outside, which made him even thirstier. He drank in small, rapid sips. When he had finished it, he put the glass carefully down on the counter, placed a twenty-euro note beside it, and stared at the bill without a word.

"Let's try again today," she said. "Please, let's try again today."

"What?" he said, still staring at the pale-blue bill, which was moving slightly in the draft of air.

"I think it will be all right today. I'm sure it will be all right."

"You are?"

"Yes. I really want to. I don't know when I last wanted to so much."

She pressed close to him again and ran her hand under his jacket. She passed it over his chest and stomach slowly and provocatively, and she didn't mind the way his sweaty shirt clung to his upper body. But he did. He moved away from her, picked up the bill, and told the waiter he wanted to pay.

The waiter didn't hear him. He was standing on the other side of the dark, shiny counter, looking toward him, and still polishing glasses. The waiter often failed to hear; that was why many customers didn't come back, but many came back for that very reason. Himself, he came here because his office was in the same building, and she often killed time in Maximilianstrasse in the afternoons.

"Right, let's not, then," she said.

"The check," he said.

The waiter put the last glass on the shelf and turned to the cash register. He had to wait, because another waiter was at the cash register, and while he waited he turned and looked briefly at the two of them. Then he told his colleague, "I think he'll make out today. I guess he'll get her into bed today." The other man grinned, but the small black-haired waiter didn't grin, he made out their bill and put it down in front of them.

She slipped off the stool and took a couple of steps to the door. She stopped in the doorway, her slender, upright figure standing out against the sunlight as if in silhouette.

He went on sitting at the bar. He stared up at the TV screen, but he had no idea what he saw there. He thought, I ought to have stayed in Georgetown with Marcia, I'd have cheated on her now and then and she'd have cheated on me, but we'd have been happy all the same, and Frederic wouldn't be a soldier now, I'd have made sure of that. She thought: He's so old and so slow, why do I love him?

He was still staring up at the screen, and then the small black-haired waiter reached up, turned the TV off, and said, "She's waiting for you."

"Yes," he said, "she's waiting for me."

He got off the bar stool, wheezing quietly, and he hoped no one had heard him wheezing.

"Well?" he said when he was beside her. He put his hand on her back, and she reacted at once and walked away.

"Well," he repeated, "what shall we do now?"

"Anything you like," she said.

He smiled, and then they went out through the curtain of sunlight, and the small black-haired waiter bent over the bar and began slicing limes for the first mojito of the evening.

Aviva's Back

It had been snowing all night and all day. Aviva stood by the open balcony door and put her head out. It was already dark, but the light of the streetlamps shone on the snow, and the snow glowed a soft, sad blue. Arkonaplatz was quieter than usual, and when a car drove past it was like the sound of a piece of fabric being slowly torn.

"Papa," said Aviva sternly, "is there someone coming to visit today?"

"What?" I said.

"I think she has black hair and glasses."

"Darling, do please come in."

"I'm not cold."

"Aviva!"

I went across the living room, quickly picked her up, and closed the balcony door behind us. Then I carried her to the bathroom.

"It's our day today," I said, while I undressed her. "Understand?"

She nodded and lay down on the floor, and I had to pull at the toes of her stockings. Their legs stretched longer and longer, and Aviva was in fits of laughter. Then she jumped up and ran away, and I found her behind the kitchen door. We looked at each other, but all the same she said, "Boo!" and I said, "No, you didn't scare me."

At that moment the telephone rang. It was Aviva's mother. They talked for a little while, and in the end Aviva looked inquiringly at me, but I shook my head. After she had finished the call she said, "Mama just wanted to know if you like the present."

I picked up the phone, called Agnes, and thanked her. While we were talking Aviva disappeared again, and I heard her turning on the shower by herself and brushing her teeth. After that she ran barefoot around my study, where she slept when she came from Frankfurt to visit, and took a great leap into bed. The bed banged against the wall, and now it was as quiet in my apartment as outside.

Instead of going in to see her I sat down in the kitchen and lit a cigarette. I was very tired. Only when Aviva was with me did I get to feel as tired as that. My whole body ached with weariness, and I thought: When can I finally get a good rest, when will she leave, when will she come back again? I smoked, and hoped for a miracle every time I drew on the cigarette. Only smokers know that feeling: you inhale, hot smoke shoots into your lungs, and you think, Any moment now everything will be different, or better, or something anyway.

When I had finished my cigarette I went quietly through the apartment and took a cautious look into the study. Aviva was almost asleep already. She was resting her head on the book I was supposed to be reading aloud to her. Her red locks covered the pages, but in between them I could see the red mane and big eyes of the Happy Lion. I watched Aviva for a while—and felt nothing. You don't always have to feel something at the sight of your child, I told myself, and then the doorbell rang. Aviva started, she opened her eyes and said, "You must tell me tomorrow if she really does have black hair and glasses, okay?" She put her head down on the book again and yawned like a little puppy.

"Happy birthday," said Joanne in English. She did have black hair, but she wasn't wearing glasses, at least not today. She looked as tired as usual, and as sexy and as strange.

"Hello," I said. "You're here?"

She stood in the doorway looking embarrassed, turning slightly away, and with something in her hand that looked like a present.

I'm the one who ought to be embarrassed, I thought, and I said in English, "My daughter's visiting."

"Oh, lovely," she said, also in English. "For how long?"

I turned without a word and went into the kitchen, without closing the front door. I fetched the cigarettes, took two bottles of beer out of the refrigerator, opened them, and went into the living room. Joanne was standing at the balcony door exactly where Aviva had been just now, looking at the empty, snow-covered square.

"Beautiful, isn't it?" she said.

"Yes," I said.

I smoked, and every time I drew on my cigarette it hurt.

"I'll be all right," she said.

"Are you sure?"

"No."

She was still standing with her back to me. She had a beautiful, almost masculine back.

"By night the snow in Washington Square is lilac colored," she said.

"Really?"

"Yes, and there are people everywhere. Always, at this time of year."

"Not like here?" I said.

"No, not like here."

"Do you want to go back?"

"No."

"Are you sure?"

"Yes."

I came up behind her, but I didn't embrace her.

"Where is he?" I said.

"Not there."

"Please, Mr. DJ, play that song," I said, and it didn't sound in the least ridiculous.

"He's in Cologne tonight, then in Nuremberg. And then in Sindeldingen or whatever it's called."

"Sindelfingen."

"That's probably it."

Now, I thought. Now you put your hand on her back, now you move it over her hip to her stomach, now you draw her close. And then I did exactly that. I kissed her throat and closed my eyes, and suddenly I saw his black, strange face. Lanois was a black man from Haiti or Jamaica, I always mixed them up. It seemed to me a little dangerous that he came from Jamaica or Haiti, and Haiti seemed a little more dangerous than Jamaica.

Since Lanois arrived from New York three weeks ago I'd seen nothing but black men around where I lived. Once I sat in Starbucks for almost half an hour beside one of them, who kept phoning his girlfriend to tell her how to get there. He spoke English like Bob Marley, and I felt sure he was Lanois, but in the end of course a woman who wasn't Joanne arrived. Next day I followed a small, attractive black man in a Stüssy hat from Weinmeisterstrasse to Alexanderplatz. He noticed me, took fright, and disappeared into the Hertie department store, where I lost him.

"Papa, are you thirty-eight or thirty-nine after today?"

I let go of Joanne at once.

Aviva was in the living room doorway, standing on one leg like a stork.

I immediately felt tired again, I felt like shouting at Aviva. Go to bed, I felt like shouting, Get out, let me get my life back in order! And she would have cried, or shouted back, or something, and I wouldn't have minded.

"Thirty-eight, poppet . . . why aren't you asleep?"

"I was thinking about this and that," she said, sounding grown up.

"Hello," said Joanne in German. "You must be Aviva."

"Hm," said Aviva.

"I'm Joanne."

"Have you been to see Papa before?"

"Yes."

"You don't have glasses. I thought you'd have glasses."

"I do, in my purse. Do you want to see them?"

"You look like an American Indian."

"My father is an American Indian."

"Is that why you speak such funny German?"

I raised my hand.

"Aviva," I said, "please."

She turned and ran into her room, crying. This time the bed didn't bang against the wall. I followed her and sat down beside her. She turned her head away, and I began stroking her back under her nightdress. As I did so I thought of Joanne's back, and I wondered whether Lanois liked it as much as I did. They'd known each other far longer than she and I had, and perhaps he'd had enough of Joanne's back by now. Perhaps he'd had enough of *her* by now too, and she'd had enough of him, but they still needed a little more of each other.

It was almost twelve when I woke up. I looked at Aviva's pink wristwatch and rubbed my face and forehead in alarm. Aviva was asleep, her mouth slightly open, which wasn't an attractive sight, but her eyes and face were relaxed, and that suited her very well. She looked like my mother and my sister, and Aya, the daughter of my sister who lives in Nahariya.

Joanne was lying on the sofa in the living room, smoking and looking out the window. She was wearing only a white undershirt and her skirt. I lay down beside her without saying a word. She turned, I pushed her skirt up and undid my trousers, and she didn't even manage to stub her cigarette out first.

"Is it different with me from with him?" I said.

She pushed me angrily away.

"Tell me."

"Stop it."

"How much longer is he staying?"

"Until we know if I still love him or not."

Good God, I thought.

She got up and went into the bathroom. She spent a long time in the bathroom, and while she was still in there Aviva woke up again. She came into the living room and lay down on the sofa with me, and luckily I was dressed again. She was so tired she could hardly speak. When I carried her back to bed, she said, "Papa, you must always live alone, okay?"

In the bathroom, Joanne was crying. I'd never heard her cry before, there was only one time when I'd thought: Now she's going to cry. That was in her gallery near the rail station, the Ostbahnhof. She'd sold three pictures to someone in Miami, and he had called to say he wasn't going to buy them after all. It would have been the first big deal she'd done in Germany. After she had hung up she began grinding her teeth like a man. She marched up and down the gallery, and when a suburban train went by overhead she screamed as loud as Liza Minnelli in *Cabaret*. Then she smiled, a chilly, crooked smile, and it was over.

I sat down in the kitchen, lit a cigarette, and waited to hear if she'd start screaming now. The picture Aviva had painted me for my birthday was lying on the table, under a pile of felt pens. It showed two dolphins leaping out of the sea and an empty beach, that was all. Above it, she had written: "BEECH." I wondered whether the picture meant anything, but probably not. What picture would I have painted today if I could paint? Something with snow in it, a great deal of snow covering a big city, and the sky would have been lilac or blue-gray, and there'd have been some stick figures with their heads in huge snowdrifts, and my caption would have been: "WHY?"

After Joanne had left I tidied up the kitchen and the living room. Then I unwrapped her present. It was a book of the photographs of Boris Mikhailov. I leafed quickly through it, once, and put it on the stack of old newspapers. I hated Boris Mikhailov—he took pictures of sick, drunk Ukrainians, mostly half naked, and I didn't understand how anyone could like his photos. Joanne liked them very much, I knew. And she had written in the book saying so too. *Something I really like. J.*

Good God, I thought, repelled, and I lit another cigarette. It was the first cigarette of the day that I enjoyed.

It's a
Sad Story

"Hello," he said, and as always he thought his voice sounded too high-pitched. "Hello, who is it?"

"I'm pregnant," said the voice at the other end of the line. It was the voice of a young woman, perhaps just a girl.

"You're pregnant?" he said.

"Yes," she said.

He was surprised, but pulled himself together at once. "I see. So how far on are you?" he said.

"In the fifth month."

"The fifth month?"

"Yes, the fifth."

He imagined her belly, and wondered whether she was lying and wanted to arouse him that way.

"Is your belly big yet?" he said.

"No."

"It isn't?"

"Well, a bit big."

"Does your boyfriend like your big belly?"

"No."

"No?"

"I don't have a boyfriend."

So that was it.

"Are you unhappy?" he said, and before she could answer he pressed zero and she was cut off. He heard music, the music they'd been playing on this line for years while you waited for the next woman. Then there was sudden silence.

"Hello," he said into the silence. "Who's there?"

"Nora. My name is Nora."

She had a deep, confident voice. It was a beautiful voice, and she certainly wouldn't be as beautiful as her voice. Or maybe she was after all.

"Are you really called Nora?"

"No. What about you?"

"My name is Ofer. I mean . . ."

". . . it isn't really Ofer."

They laughed.

If you laughed with them you always got quite a long way. Well, he thought, it wasn't all that different in real life.

"I know you," she said.

"No, I'm sure you don't."

"I do. I know your voice."

"What have you been doing today?" he asked.

"Nothing. I never do anything . . . I do know your voice."

"Perhaps we've spoken on this line before."

"No," she said, "today is my first time."

He moved farther up in bed, put the second pillow under his head, and turned the covers back in anticipation.

"What do you look like?" he asked.

"You wouldn't like me."

"Aren't you pretty?"

"No." She said that very quickly and with conviction, as if she'd already said so, and thought it, a thousand times before. "No."

He knew that "no." It was not the "no" of someone pathetically ugly, it was the "no" of a beautiful woman who had to keep being told how beautiful she was, or else she didn't believe it.

"I don't believe you," he said. He paused for a moment, and then said, "I like you."

"How can you know that?" she said.

"Don't *you* ever know when you like something?" he said.

"Yes, of course I do."

Then there was suddenly nothing more to say. They fell silent, and his finger was already hovering over the zero to get rid of her when she said, "What do you do?"

"I'm a boxer."

"Really?"

"No. That was just nonsense."

"Me, I lie in bed all day," she said.

"Do you?"

"Yes."

"Are you lying in bed now too?"

"Yes, now too."

"I'm already lying down," he said, and he began unbuttoning his pajama top. When he had undone all the buttons he covered himself up. He felt the quilt on his bare chest, and it was as if he were not alone in his bed, and another naked body would be pressing close to his the next moment.

"That can't be right. You don't really lie in bed all day," he said.

"Yes, I do."

"Don't you have to go to work?"

"No, I don't."

"Why not?" he said, feeling excited. So she was not just beautiful, she was wealthy too.

"I'm sick."

"Really?"

"Yes."

"You're sick, are you?"

"Yes."

"And your husband . . ."

"My lover."

". . . your lover goes out to work."

"Yes."

"And he's never there."

"I *have* heard you before," she said.

He pressed zero, and as soon as he had pressed zero he regretted it. What did she mean, she was sick? Did she have only one leg? Was she depressive? Was she slowly dying of a tumor? Well, it was none of his business.

He stayed on the line for a few more minutes, but the two of them were not connected again. Twice running he found himself talking to aggressive, laughing teenagers who called him obscene names, and then the pregnant woman was back on the line still looking for a father for her baby.

He ended the call, buttoned his pajamas again, and went in to Felix.

As usual, the child had turned over in bed and was lying on his back, arms outspread as if he were falling. His little face was relaxed in sleep, the lines had disappeared from his forehead, and you might think everything in his life was in order. Ofer—his name really was Ofer—opened the window and sat down on Felix's bed. He looked at the floor and shook his head a couple of times, then he kissed the boy and went back to his own bed.

He lay in bed, trying to get to sleep and thinking of dead Katia. In the end he switched the light on again, called the same number as before, and she was the very first woman he was connected to.

"Hello, Ofer," she said firmly.

"Oh, hello," he said, and acted surprised. "Hello, Nora."

"Why did you cut us off?"

"It was a mistake," he said. "Or no—it wasn't a mistake."

"I'm plump, but not too plump," she said. "I have small breasts but a big bum. Do you like big bums?"

"Please stop it."

"Isn't this what you want?"

"No."

"The others all do. I had four . . . no, three, while you were off the line."

"You had them—or they had you?"

"They had me."

He switched off the bedside lamp and settled comfortably. He lay on his side with the receiver beneath his ear on the pillow, so that he didn't have to hold it.

"The worst thing is the silence," she said. "All day long, when there's no one there. The whole building is empty, everyone's at work. And I lie in my bed waiting to hear something. Once a week I hear the cleaning lady in the apartment above us. She rushes frantically back and forth, and when she runs the vacuum cleaner over the wooden flooring it squeals. When the heating comes on in the cellar there's a hissing in the radiators, dying down until it stops entirely. And in the building next door there's an answering machine, I hear that too. Sometimes it startles me. It's a very loud answering machine."

"It is?"

"Yes. I can hear every word it says. I've been hearing it for years, and I always know what's going on at my neighbors'. It's funny, they never change their message. As if life were always the same."

"What *is* going on at your neighbors'?"

"It's a sad story."

"Then I don't want to hear it."

"I won't tell it, then."

"Nora."

"Yes?"

"Tell me what you look like again."

"You didn't want to know."

"But now I do."

"Oh, no."

"No?"

"No."

"Okay. Perhaps you're right. Maybe . . ."

"Maybe it's better this way?" she interrupted him.

"Yes."

"Maybe. Or maybe not."

What were they to talk about now? They were silent, but it was not an awkward silence. He didn't feel that she was about to cut him off, and he didn't want to press zero either. He heard her breathing, he was breathing louder and louder himself, and for a while they breathed in time.

"Where's your lover?" he said. "It's late."

"He isn't here."

"He works very hard."

"Yes—at two in the morning."

"Is that so?"

"Yes."

Ofer closed his eyes, and the large bright circles turning behind his eyelids reminded him of the past. In the past, when he was Felix's age, he often lay in bed for half an hour, a whole hour, forcing himself not to fall asleep and watching the beautiful shining circles behind his lids.

"How long have you been sick?" he asked.

"Not long enough for him to dare to leave me yet."

"Will he leave you?"

"No, I don't think so."

"You're contradicting yourself."

"Yes," she said.

"Why won't he leave?"

"People only leave when things are too good. They don't leave to save themselves."

That's true, thought Ofer, but he said, "Nonsense," and the circles turned faster and faster and grew bigger and bigger, and he fell asleep.

"Hello, darling," he suddenly heard her voice.

He opened his eyes and quickly sat up in bed.

"Hello," he said.

"Are you still there?"

"Yes . . . yes."

"Let's go to sleep now," she said.

"When will we speak again?" he said.

"Tomorrow, if you like."

"When tomorrow?"

"At the same time."

"We might not get connected."

"Could that happen?"

"Anything can happen. So many men call the number."

"I'll find you all the same," she said. Her voice was friendly but a little too forthcoming, and he took fright.

"You will?" he said.

"Yes," she said. "I told you, I know your voice."

"Do you know where from?"

"Yes."

He jumped out of bed and put the main light on. He walked up and down in the bedroom, constantly pushing aside the two chairs that were in his way.

"Where from, then?" he said.

"You won't want to know."

"Yes, I will. Why not?"

"No, it would be better not to tell you."

"Tell me."

"Hello," she said, imitating his own Jewish singsong, "this

is the home of Katia, Felix, and Ofer Bernstein. I'm sorry, we are not here just now. Please leave a message on the answering machine."

"No," he said.

"Yes . . ."

"That's our answering machine."

"Yes," she said. "I'm sorry."

"No, never mind, it's all right," he murmured.

He ended the call, switched the light off, and got into bed. Curled up like a baby, he lay awake half the night. When he finally dropped off to sleep it was already light. Half an hour later Felix got into bed with him and said he wanted to watch videos.

Yellow Sandals

For an Iranian she was rather too large, but she had beautiful little feet. They were not too small, they were quite long, which he liked, and if you looked down at them from above they were almost an identical trapezoid shape. Best of all were her toes. Two sets of five lovely peach-brown toes, slender, long, the two big toes with that coquettish, waisted look you so seldom saw, strong and rounded farther forward, so you knew what you had there when you took them in your mouth.

She had simply stayed sitting beside him one evening. It was in Mánes, where the tables and chairs were still from the pre-revolutionary period, and so were the waiters. They were sitting together on the black leather sofa, which was too low, the others were talking about the conference and the minister of culture's beard, and Sonya and he were talking about Sonya's father or looking out at the waters of the Vltava. The river was black, with small, pale crests of foam surfacing here and there, to be swallowed up again at once by the dark water. The yellow and blue lights of Smíchov were reflected in the water. Sometimes a party boat passed by, rocking violently, and when almost everyone else had left he kissed her. After pressing her shoulder repeatedly against his, she kept her face close to his face, he kissed her, and was surprised to find how simple it all was.

Now she was lying under him, he was holding her firmly by the ankles and taking her toes in his mouth one by one, and he had his eyes open and so did she. It's always the same, he thought. It's like *Groundhog Day* where that nice actor— what was his name?—keeps waking up in the same horrible small town every morning, it's always the same morning, the radio is playing Sonny & Cher, at least I've remembered that now, but I wish I knew the name of the song. It's always the same, I talk to them, I talk and talk, I listen to the troubles they haven't told anyone about for a long time, they look searchingly into my eyes and I look innocently back, or maybe not quite so innocently, and it's that look that has them undressing for me only a few hours later. It really is always the same. In the end I'm left lying on top of them, exhausted, I kiss them listlessly on the throat and hold them tight, although I'd rather not, and then I go to wash myself, but if they too want to wash I feel just a little insulted. After that we sleep side by side, we wake up, it's morning, I go into the bathroom again, and when I come back the smell of the bedroom tells me that I absolutely must spend the next night alone. It's always the same.

He sat up with a jerk and let go of her feet.

"Something wrong?" she said in English.

"Oh, no, no," he said, and he thought: Concentrate, or no—even better, don't concentrate.

"Okay," she said, as if it were a question, and smiling put her hand down between herself and him. At first it was pleasant, then it hurt, then it was pleasant again. He looked at her almost lovingly and saw her long, pale-brown upper body, her breasts with nipples that were a little too dark, her sweeping, beautiful collarbone, her long throat, her grave face surrounded by a profusion of black hair, then he drew her feet toward him again and began heaping kisses on each in turn. She watched him, and when he looked back at her she sighed softly, and he thought, Maybe she's the one.

He thought, Yes, why not, why not her? She lives in the States, but that's no problem, I like the States, or not the States but New York. I've always been happy in New York, perhaps I'll be happy in Philadelphia where she lives. What's Philadelphia like? There's that movie with Tom Hanks—ah, I'm glad I remembered the name of Tom Hanks right away—and it's set in Philadelphia, and Tom Hanks is terribly sick, I even remember why, oh, God, better not think of that, but how are we going to do this without a condom, how are we going to manage? Better not think of that, I just mustn't forget to pull out, I never asked if she was taking anything, but if she does get pregnant by me, well, yes, why not?

"Don't come inside me," she said. She said it gently but firmly. She pressed against him as if she were the man and he the woman, as if she were in him and not he in her. He returned her pressure, but she was stronger, and perhaps he was just being polite enough not to make much of it just now.

I still have her feet, he thought. He pushed her legs together, her feet were moving in the air, and he rubbed his cheeks against her soft, pink soles while she went on pressing against him. He kissed every square centimeter of her soles, he nibbled her heels, and began thinking again. He thought, Will it always be like this for us when we're living in Philadelphia, will we always sleep together like this? He saw a dark little room in a small brownstone, there were tall, dark trees outside, and the Virginia creeper climbing all over the house even grew into the dark little room. From a distance, he saw her and himself lying there, she lay like a letter L, on her back on the bed, legs together and up in the air, he was kneeling in front of her in an L shape too, like an L in reverse, and he thought: I hope her father doesn't come in now.

Why, he wondered, do I think of her father at this moment? Because she was telling me so much about him in

Mánes? She said he was never satisfied with her, he was always saying she was sexy and there was nothing else to her, but she had studied and worked for all she was worth, and now she was deputy to her boss at the ITC, and she'd soon be boss herself, but if Daddy comes in now he'll just say yet again, "See, that's all you can do," and I don't want to be there when that happens, I really don't.

He stopped, and for a moment he didn't know where he was. Then he did know again. He wasn't in Philadelphia, he was in Prague, in his bedroom on Lucemburská Street, it was three in the morning, and outside the window stood the tall, silver television tower that looked, in the white spotlights, like a spaceship about to take off. Back when it was built his parents and the neighbors had campaigned against the Communists putting up the tower right in the middle of a residential district, because of the radiation and the Jewish cemetery below it, but that didn't interest the Communists. He himself loved the sight of the tower. He looked out at it now, and she looked out with him and put her hand down between him and herself again. Then she held him to her even more tightly, she threw her arms apart and pulled at the sheet and sighed twice out loud, and that was it.

Now what? He stared at her in surprise, and tried to go on, but it was as if she just wasn't there anymore. She wearily put her arms around his torso as he bent over her, embraced her, and went on moving pointlessly back and forth. Then she slipped away from him, knocked her head on the wall as she did so, said, "Ouch!" and rolled over on her side, with her back to him.

"Did I hurt you?" he asked.

"No."

"Sure?"

"Yes. I'm fine." She turned around, and as he was still kneeling on the bed she looked up at him. She stroked his thighs and said, "Sweetie, I really have to go now."

She stood up and slowly began to dress, and she didn't seem happy.

She isn't going to wash, he thought. She already has her panties and bra on, now she's pulling up the zipper of her skirt, she's twisting the skirt around so that the zipper is at the back, of course, that's what I'd do too, but where's her T-shirt, here's her T-shirt, it was in the bed between the covers, is she really not going to wash?

He lay on his back and watched her, and when she had finished dressing she put the main light on and looked for her shoes. She had been wearing yellow sandals with high heels, he remembered that. He had stared at them in Mánes and also in the Rudolfinum during the speeches, and those yellow sandals were the last things he had taken off her earlier. They must be somewhere in the bed, but they weren't—one was under the radiator, the other on the windowsill. She put them on standing, and bent quickly to fasten the buckles, then she looked at him gravely and with a touch of dislike, and she simply left.

He heard her open the front door of the apartment and close it quietly after her. She went downstairs, and through the open living room window he could still hear the click-clack of her high heels on the sidewalk for a while. The click-clack died away, and at last all was perfectly quiet again in this part of the city. He closed his eyes and thought of her small, peach-colored feet, thought of them walking fast and alone away through Prague on a summer night, going away from him, and sad as it made him feel, he could well understand those small, peach-colored feet.

Ziggy Stardust

Once I thought, I don't want to go on. That's some time ago now. My new book had just been published, a love story set among young Nazis. I'd written it fast, it came out and was immediately banned. Only a few people had read it, and one of them was Edna.

I'd known Edna since I was ten. She and her parents lived around the corner from us, in Schlüterstrasse, and I'd sometimes seen her going out to tennis practice in her tennis things. She was a serious girl whose mind was always somewhere else. Her eyes were blue and empty, and her lips a little like mine. Now and then she smiled when we met in the street, but the smile wasn't for me.

I never thought about Edna at the time. Like me, she came

from a Jewish family, but theirs was rather complicated. That was why Edna seldom went to synagogue. Her father came from Hungary and wasn't Jewish, or perhaps he was after all and didn't want to be anymore. That sort of thing often happened after the war.

But the Radvanyis always went to synagogue on the religious holidays in autumn. Edna sat by the window in the ugly outer hall with her grave little father beside her, she leaned her head on his shoulder or laid it on his lap. Her mother, who was even smaller than her father, stayed in the main hall until the end of the service, and when everyone came out after it she went up to her husband and her daughter, smiling, kissed them both, and said quietly, *"Chag sameach."* I liked that, but something made me uneasy when I saw the three of them together.

One year it rained in buckets. It was the end of Yom Kippur and I was in the synagogue on my own, because my parents had to go to Israel on business concerning our hotel. Almost everyone had left already. I stood in the doorway, the young Israeli security man was shifting restlessly from foot to foot beside me, and suddenly I heard Edna's voice behind me. "My mother says you can come and have supper with us, then you won't be on your own." I turned, and Edna quickly passed me. She had put her umbrella up, I ran after her, and got into her parents' car with her.

After supper we went into Edna's room. She played me her records, and we sat side by side on her bed in silence, listening to them. A large butterfly poster from the Friedrichsruh butterfly garden hung above Edna's desk, and there were butterfly stickers on the lamp and her large white wardrobe.

Edna had David Bowie's *Ziggy Stardust* and *Hunky Dory*, and a lot of French records that I didn't know. I told her I liked *Ziggy Stardust* best, and she said I could have the record, she couldn't take it with her anyway.

"Is your family moving?" I asked.

"No," she said.

"What is it, then?"

"I'm going to be away for some time," she said, "and there's no record player there."

"Are you going abroad?"

"No," she said.

"Well, I'll give you back the record as soon as you come home," I said.

"Don't bother about that," she said.

After that I didn't see Edna for almost two years. I asked my parents if they knew anything about her, and they said no. Perhaps they really did know something, in fact I'm sure they did, but they don't like gossip, and I asked no more questions.

I met Edna again at the big tennis tournament in the Rotherbaum district. I'd been given a free ticket by a guest of my parents, and I knew that Edna used to be a ball girl here with the others from her club. She was too old for that these days. She was sitting near the drink kiosk outside the Center Court along with a group of rich young Germans. She had beautiful breasts now, and she wore her straight dark hair a little like Daliah Lavi.

She was on the edge of the group, and a small black-haired man with his sunglasses pushed up and a port-wine stain on his cheek was talking quietly to her. I said hello, and she looked at me in surprise. So did all the rest of them at her table. We talked for a moment or two, and finally I asked if she'd like me to stop by with her record. She didn't mind, she said, and she seemed glad when I left.

That evening, quite late, our doorbell rang. It was Edna. She said she'd like to have the record back after all, and while she waited for me in the living room I went to look for it. It didn't take me long. When I came back Edna was standing by the open balcony door. The cold wind was blowing in, and there was a smell of fall in the air.

"Do you feel like going for a walk?" she said, turning to me.

I shrugged my shoulders. "Why not?" I said. "Though I was really about to go to bed."

We walked to the river Alster, where we sat down on a bench in spite of the cold and looked at the city on the other side. Then we went into the kiosk looking out on the Alster, drank tea, and quite soon walked back again. I didn't talk much and Edna said almost nothing. She touched my hand once, probably just by chance.

We said good-bye outside Edna's door. I wondered whether to kiss her. In those days I wanted to kiss almost every girl. At our hotel in Herzliya I even almost slept with my little cousin Jessy from Long Island once, just because it would have been so easy. But I didn't kiss Edna, I quickly went away. Not until I found her David Bowie record on our living room sofa at home did I think of Edna again, and then I realized what I'd missed.

Whenever Edna and I met by chance over the next few years we talked. I knew what was the matter with her now. I didn't mind. I didn't feel particularly sorry for her, but it didn't scare me either. Usually I feel uncomfortable with people who have problems of that kind, because I'm afraid they might be infectious. It wasn't like that with Edna, and sometimes I thought of calling her and going to a film with her.

Later, when I'd moved away from Hamburg, we saw each other again from time to time. She seemed to be all right now. She came to the readings I gave in Hamburg, and stayed with the rest of us afterward when we went out to eat. She always came, and I always exchanged a few words with her, but there were other people there who mattered more to me. She was never pushy and usually she left quite early, but the next time she would turn up again.

Once—this was in Cuneo—I was coming back from the men's room and met her at the door. She had her coat on, and a cap, and a thick green scarf around her neck.

"Leaving already?" I said.

"Yes," she said.

"That's a pity."

"Yes."

"Stay a little longer."

"No."

"Well, suit yourself. Are you okay?"

"Yes, I'm fine."

"Good."

She smiled abstractedly, and suddenly there she was again—the girl coming toward me across the Hallerplatz in her tennis things. We kissed good-bye on both cheeks, and I went back to my table.

After that Edna and I didn't see each other for a long time. I wondered if she was in a sanatorium again, or if she'd married. Last time we met she'd told me she was going to go on a civil service training course in New York, perhaps she'd stayed there. When I was leafing through American journals in editorial offices I often looked at the photos in the gossip columns, hoping to find her there. After a while I stopped doing that.

When I threw out my record player and sold all the records, I didn't stop to think that one of them was Edna's *Ziggy Stardust*. The boy in the record shop in Danziger Strasse who was looking through the box took the red and blue record out at once and said he'd like to keep it himself, if that was all right. I said of course, but a few weeks later I went to Dussmann and bought it on CD. Once home I put it on before I'd even taken my coat off. After two or three songs I turned it off again, and stored it with the less important CDs.

I'd almost forgotten Edna by the time we next met, years

later. It was at Rosh Hashanah in the Hamburg synagogue. She and her mother were coming down from upstairs while I and my father waited for my mother. Edna's eyes were different, I noticed that at once. She was a woman now, with attractive lines around her mouth and eyes, and looking into those new, different eyes I thought, I want to know what she knows. I think she knew that too. Although her mother and my father were standing there with us, acting as if they didn't mind in the least when their grown-up children would finally find someone to marry, we made a date for the next evening right in front of them.

Edna had read my book, the one that was banned. "I read your book," she said. "You wrote it too fast." She also thought she could understand why everyone had been so upset about it. "Especially the old Nazis, because they don't come into it at all."

Edna was much more amusing than before. We laughed when we stood side by side in the bathroom at night, cleaning our teeth; we laughed when we quarrelled, we laughed when we discussed her moodiness and my know-it-all attitude. We even laughed when she told me about her father's parents, who had only just made it to Poland in time on the last transport from Hungary.

"Don't look like that—as if you'd been standing in that train yourself," I said when she'd finished.

"Sitting," she said.

"Sitting, standing, what's the difference?"

"Well, imagine arriving in Auschwitz with a pain in the small of your back to make things even worse!"

It was Sunday morning, and we were in bed at my place in Berlin. The sun shone into the bedroom and warmed our bare backs.

"Now?" I said.

"Now."

"Without kissing?"

"With."

"No, without."

"No, with."

"Without."

"Oh, all right."

I put my arms around her, and when I couldn't think very straight anymore she kissed me all the same.

"You tricked me," I said.

"We have the same mouth," she said. "Do you know that?"

"Can we please finish one thing before we discuss another?"

"No."

"Very well, then."

"Very well what?"

"Yes, we do have the same mouth."

"Why aren't you going on?"

"What?"

"Oh, come on, get on with it."

We saw each other almost every weekend. Either she came to Berlin or I went to Hamburg. When we didn't see each other we phoned. We phoned several times a day, we often sent each other text messages, we exchanged emails. By mail, I sent Edna the flower photos I'd been taking for years. She sent me pictures of herself as a child, or her photos of buildings and streets in Israel. Once she sent me a series of pictures she'd taken in a beautiful old house in the country. It could have been in Bavaria or Switzerland, or maybe England. It was the same view every time, seen from a window, a view of a park with a large empty lawn. There were some old trees to the right and left of the lawn, probably chestnuts, I wasn't quite sure. You saw the park in winter, in summer; in the morning, at midday, by night. Sometimes snow had fallen, sometimes the lawn was covered with dark leaves. I knew what the place was without having to ask Edna. And she knew that I knew.

"Ariel," said Edna one day, "I don't know if I'm going to make it."

"I do," I said.

"I want to make it, though."

"I know, darling."

"But suppose *you* don't make it?"

"That could happen too, of course," I said.

"No, I don't think so," she said.

"Are you sure?"

"Netanyahu was on the BBC yesterday."

"What?"

"Netanyahu."

"So?"

"I think he's sexy."

"I thought you didn't like him."

"I don't, but he knows what he wants, and he does as he likes, and he doesn't mind what other people think of it."

We were walking through the city center of Hamburg; it was raining slightly. Then it stopped raining and the sun came out. Its rays were reflected in the shopwindows here and there, and when you looked into them you blinked in surprise.

I had fetched Edna from her office at the Neuer Wall. I always felt a little uncomfortable seeing her with her colleagues. She laughed and talked to them in the same way as she did with me, and didn't notice how odd these large, serious people thought her and her jokes. I told her so when we were sitting in the Bar Tabac in the Galleria later, smoking the first cigarette of the day. But she only said, "Of course I notice, you idiot." And then she said. "What shall we do today?"

We went to the DOM carnival. We didn't really like the place. "But then, we live here," said Edna in the car. She wanted to have a go at the shooting gallery and then leave again. She said you had to breathe right in and hold your breath before firing, then you couldn't miss. She hit the target every time, but she didn't want the large, fluffy orange fish that she won.

Then it was my turn. There were butterflies, and since she liked butterflies and had some old glass cases of butterfly collections in her apartment I wanted to win her a butterfly. I breathed right in, held my breath, fired—and missed. I did that five times, ten times, by then I was nervous about it, but I couldn't stop. Edna said that with me as a sharpshooter in an Israeli helicopter, half the Hamas casualties would still be alive, and the old man with two missing front teeth who was loading my rifle said, You sound very militant, young lady. Does that bother you? she asked, and he said, Far from it, and she said, A real man at last. He laughed, and she laughed too; I said, I'd like to concentrate again, please, but they went on laughing all the same, I fired, and finally I hit the target.

The butterfly I'd won for Edna wasn't very large. It was made of fabric and wire, it had blue and yellow wings and a safety pin at the back. Edna pinned it to her jacket, she kissed me on the cheek and took my arm. We walked quickly back through the carnival to her car. There was a lot of noise, you heard German hit songs and hip-hop on all sides. Sad young people pushed past in small groups, and the thousands of lights around us made none of it any better.

Suddenly Edna stopped and said, "Hello."

"Hello," said a man of about my own age. He had wavy black hair, like me, and he wore the same kind of large horn-rimmed glasses, rather too large for him. He looked like a German copy of me. Beside him stood a very sweet-looking little blond woman. She was smiling prettily.

"This is Sebastian," said Edna. She coughed. Then she said, "This is Ariel."

"I'm Inken," said the blonde.

"Inken?" I said.

"That's right, Inken."

We stood there for a little while in silence, and Sebastian told Inken, "This is Edna."

"I know," said Inken.

"You do?" said Edna.

"Yes."

"So where have you two been?" asked Edna.

"We've only just arrived."

"We're just going."

"What else were you planning to do?"

"We haven't decided."

There was another silence.

"Imagine you being here at all," said Sebastian to Edna. He went red.

"Have a good time, then," said Edna, drawing me away by my arm.

"You too," Inken told us. Sebastian said nothing more at all.

"Have a good time?" I said, when we were finally in the car, driving back to Edna's. I laughed, but I wasn't feeling good, and I felt like a liar who mustn't tell lies.

Edna didn't reply. She looked straight ahead down the street, and I knew what kind of expression there was in her eyes just now. But then—we were waiting at the big Grindelhof traffic lights—she turned to me, grinned, and said, "Well, let's see what else we can get up to, *yachabibi*."

About a month later Edna disappeared. She was supposed to be arriving in Berlin one Friday afternoon, and she called in the morning to say she'd be leaving rather later than planned. She sounded uneasy, but perhaps I only imagined that later. I waited for her until early evening and then went to the Friedrichshain public park. I sat down on the grass, smoked, and watched a few men of my own age playing football. It was one of the first really warm evenings of the year, the ground wasn't cold or damp, and it didn't get dark until late. After a while I fell asleep. When I woke up it was black all around me, and I was alone in the park. I looked at my phone, but no message had come in. I smoked another cigarette and slowly went home. She wasn't there either.

I woke up very early the next morning. As usual, I hadn't been dreaming, but while I was still lying there drowsily with my face in the pillows, I saw Edna driving down a narrow, shady country road in her car. She was driving with her eyes closed, listening to *Ziggy Stardust* at high volume, and she looked like our daughter, the one we never had. At that moment I thought I'd have to stop living. I wondered briefly how I was going to do it, then I quickly got up and went into the bathroom. I spent a long time shaving, I ate breakfast standing up, and I wrote two pages more than usual that day.

I didn't look for Edna. I never called her again, and I didn't ask anyone what had become of her. I could have talked to her mother. But when I met Frau Radvanyi at the Hackescher Markt a few months later I didn't say anything. She had come to Berlin with some relatives from Israel, an old couple who wanted to see the city again after sixty years. We talked about old Berlin, and what the place was like now. Then Edna's mother asked when my next book was coming out. Of course she could have told me what had become of Edna, if she or I had wanted—whether she wasn't very well again, or whether she was with Sebastian, or someone entirely different, or just on her own, or whatever. But she didn't.

Before we parted she squeezed my arm and said, "What a pity, Ariel."

"Please give your husband my regards, Frau Radvanyi," I said. "I mean it."

"I'll try. Sometimes he still understands what people say to him. But less and less often now."

"I'm sorry."

"Don't worry, he's all right."

She kissed me good-bye, and I shook hands with the two old Israelis. The woman was very small; she had short gray hair and a brown old face. She was edgy and not really very likeable; I took to her husband more. He wasn't much taller than her, he had the same thick, short gray hair, the same dark brown face, but unlike her he looked at me with interest. Before they disappeared in the crowd outside the S-Bahn station, he turned to look at me again. I waved, and he waved back.

The Sweet
Whore

She said she was Greek, or her father was Greek, but she'd never
seen him.

Sami didn't believe her. He was sure she was a gypsy, but
people didn't like admitting to that in Prague. All the same he said
that was great, he liked Greeks, and he told her about the Greek
restaurant on Kubelíkova Street, where he and Hans and Jocelyn
spent almost every afternoon sitting around this summer. They sat
outside in the garden by the whitewashed wall, and a large white
cat stalked along the wall, and it was as if they weren't in Prague.

"It's as if we weren't in Prague at all," Sami said.

She didn't reply.

"Have you ever been there?"

"Where?"

"It's called Olympos."

"No," she said. "I haven't been here very long. I come from Brno."

He gave her the money, and she went out to give it to the madam. When she came back he gave her another two hundred crowns.

"Thanks," she said, "but you don't have to do that."

"No?"

"No, darling."

He went to shower. Then she showered, and he sat on the bed in his undershirt and underpants and looked at the candle burning on the bedside table. A small glass dish of condoms stood beside the candle, a tube of body cream was sticking out of the half-open drawer. For a minute he didn't know where he was, and closed his eyes. Then he opened them, and everything was okay again.

It was early afternoon, the July sun was blazing down outside, but the thick green curtains were drawn. Hans and Jocelyn would be sure to be sitting in Olympos talking everything over again, and when he'd finished here he would switch on his phone and there'd be a half dozen messages from them in his mailbox. Those two just couldn't be on their own. Whenever they were on their own they went around and around in circles. When he was there they went around and around in circles too, but at least then he was turning with them. Last week they had even come to blows, and when he saw them the next day sitting in the garden of Olympos with their scratches and bruises, he said he'd rather be alone. "But you are anyway," Hans had said, and Jocelyn ran her cold hand over the back of Sami's neck and squeezed it for a moment, and they both laughed at the same time and ordered their fourth or fifth glass of wine.

Lenka let the white towel which she had wrapped around her after showering fall on the floor, and stood in front of him naked. Her skin looked even browner in the dim light of the darkened room. Her breasts were not beautiful, but her hips were full and rounded, and she'd shaved. It looked as if she'd never had any hair there at all, and he remembered that she was just eighteen and had said she'd been a working girl for only two months, since she came to Prague from Brno. Her mother hadn't wanted her to take her final school exams, and one night she had poured boiling water over her mother and ran away.

She sat down on the bed beside him, and they looked at each other. They said nothing for a while, which was very pleasant, and then she asked him why he didn't get undressed too. She lay on her back, he bent over her and put his arms around her. This wasn't the first time he'd paid for it, but he had never put his arms around one of them before. He held Lenka tight and kissed her throat and her cheeks, and when he looked at her briefly while he was kissing her, he saw that her eyes were closed and she was smiling slightly.

Hans had told him you could be lucky with these things in Prague, but he hadn't believed him. Hans had been to a gypsy girl in Blanická Street for a year. When she suddenly disappeared overnight he was in a bad way for a few weeks. That was long ago, long before Jocelyn. Now he was in a bad way again—because of Jocelyn. By now everyone at the Academy knew about them—the professor and the student!—and that made it no easier for him. He told Sami she was like a stray dog, she came only when she wanted, and she didn't trust anyone. Could be, replied Sami, but maybe she's just too fat for you. When Sami began looking at the photos of the girls in the ads and writing down their numbers, Hans had told Sami that if he found a nice one he might go there himself again.

"You're wet," said Sami.

"Yes," she said.

He caressed her between the legs and thought, She's wet.

"Why?" he asked. He raised his head and looked down at her.

"I don't know," she said.

"Are you really wet?"

"Yes," she said impatiently, rolling her eyes.

"Would you turn over, please?" he asked.

She turned over, and he looked at her from behind. Then he pressed against her, pressed his body against hers, and held her like that for a few seconds without moving. She didn't move either, and finally he told her to turn over again. Now he was kneeling in front of her. "May I come on your stomach?" he asked.

"Yes, but please be careful," she said.

When he came on her stomach she covered herself down below with one hand, and with the other she held his hand as if he were her boyfriend, or someone who was sick with a fever.

Afterward they talked again. He was in no hurry to leave her. She slowly stroked his arm, now and then unobtrusively glancing at the clock above the door. He asked how good her Greek was, but she didn't like that subject. She preferred to talk about the way German men were always trying to teach her certain German words. Or how sometimes handsome young Czechs visited, which she didn't understand. Once three of them had turned up together, and she and the other two girls here had all done it with them at the same time. She herself, she said, had snapped up the most handsome and refused to let him go.

"Would you have refused to let me go too?" said Sami, laughing.

"Of course," she said, and she laughed herself. She got up, and as she did so she turned away from him, but looking at her sideways he could see her young, happy face briefly freezing at that moment. Then she turned to him again and smiled.

"Will you come back another time?" she said as she opened the front door for him downstairs.

"Maybe," he said. He nodded to her and walked quickly away. He was in a good mood, he noticed that at once. The bright sunlight was dazzling him a little, he blinked a couple of times as if he had something in his eyes, and he thought, Better not turn around. Then he turned around after all, but she wasn't there anymore.

He switched his phone on as he walked. No call while it was turned off, no message. They probably murdered each other last night, he thought, grinning. He went on to Francouzká Street and stood at the tram stop, and as he waited for the tram to Žižkov he decided to go back to Barcelona that week. He'd been in Prague for six months, although he hadn't meant to stay for longer than a few weeks, and he was just wasting his time here, the way he did everywhere.

Dear Arthur

I had a rather difficult relationship just behind me. First I didn't want to, then she didn't want to. Then she said, "I'll write you a letter, darling, when I know what I've decided." The letter had arrived a few days ago, and now I could begin again from the beginning.

The next evening, when I arrived at Borchardt much too late, I thought: Now, that one's not bad! She was sitting at a table with Emil, and we saw each other from a distance.

Emil was still all excited because of the Horvath Prize, which had been presented to him at the Berliner Ensemble theater that morning. "Why weren't you there?" he said. His small, anxious face was as pink as the peach sorbet in front of him.

"Sorry," I said, and shook hands with him. He wanted to kiss me, because theatrical people are always kissing. So we kissed. Then I said hello to the others sitting side by side at the long table with its white cloth. Most of them I didn't know, and I thought the few I did boring.

She was still looking at me. She had the kind of eyes you call dark and interesting, and can quickly get on your nerves. And she had a very red mouth. Women with dark and interesting eyes often do, and their lipstick is usually shinier than it should be.

The eyes of the woman who wrote the letter had been different. Dark too, but different. When you looked into them you saw yourself, as long as you were with her anyway.

I pulled a chair over from another table and asked people to move up. Now we were sitting exactly opposite each other. I pressed my knee slightly against hers, and she moved away.

"What will you have to drink?" she asked.

"I don't care."

"Will you drink red wine with me?"

"No."

She laughed. She was fifteen years younger than I, and she addressed me by the formal "you" pronoun.

"Are you hungry?"

"I've been feeling unwell for days."

"Okay," she said. "I understand."

Then she told me what she was doing in Berlin—it had something to do with Emil's prize. She was going back to

Cologne the next day, and she had another twelve hours before her train left. She said so twice.

While she was talking I wondered what it would be like to rest my head on her shoulder. I wondered whether she had two little dimples at the base of her back. And then I leaned toward her to find out if I liked the smell of her.

She leaned forward too and said, "I've seen everything you did in Bochum, Arthur."

The voices around us rose. It was as if someone were slowly turning up the volume. It didn't bother me, I didn't have to hear every word she said.

Then Emil, anxious little Emil, called down the entire table, "Hi there, I'd like us all to raise a glass to Ödön!"

The waiter went around with a tray, and everyone had a glass of vodka. We drained them, and a very tall, gray-haired East German said, "And now another to Emil!"

"Why weren't you at the B.E. today?" she said.

"I'm afraid I couldn't get there."

"I think," she said, so softly that I could hardly hear her through the noise, "you ought to get the prize too."

I wondered whether to press my knee against hers again. The waiter brought new glasses, and everyone drank to Emil. As we clinked glasses we looked at each other for some time, and my eyeglasses were reflected in her pupils.

"I must leave soon," she said. "When does the last train to Wannsee go?"

"Soon, I should think," I said.

"Right," she said, "then I'd better be off now."

I felt unwell again. I thought of the last three months. It had been best when Nomi and I lay in bed one Saturday afternoon drinking tea. I lay with my head against the wall, Nomi on my other side, and she was holding the cup carefully in her hands as if it might break. We talked about her father's kiosk in Leibnizstrasse, where my sister and I always used to steal stuff when we were kids.

Someone's knee touched mine.

"Do you live far from here?" she said.

"Not too far," I said.

"Do you have a nice apartment?"

I nodded.

"What does a night's stay in your nice apartment cost?"

"What?"

"I could offer five hundred euros."

"I don't understand."

"Five hundred."

"No," I said quickly, "that wouldn't do."

"Six hundred and fifty. I really can't go any higher."

"No. Excuse me."

I stood up and went to the men's room. As I went down the stairs I was afraid of falling. As I climbed them again I pictured Nomi and me sitting at my aunt Flora's kitchen table in Haifa, eating her terrible apple cake. Flora was talking about Hungary and Auschwitz and chuckling in her high, feline voice.

"Very well," I said when I came back. "Do we leave now or later?"

She was talking to the tall East German, and I had to interrupt them.

"What?" she said.

"Very well," I said.

"I don't understand," she replied, and then she turned back to the other man. He had worked as an assistant to Besson, and she wanted to know all about it.

I sat there for a while in silence, listening to them. When she had emptied her glass I refilled it, and I gave her a light. She didn't once look at me.

When I left we shook hands. Her hand was cold and firm; I think mine was too.

"Cheer up, Arthur," cried Emil. I was already standing by the coatrack. "Next year we'll be drinking to Ödön and you here!"

I waved and went out.

Back home, I read Nomi's letter again. "Dear Arthur," she wrote, "Yesterday morning I saw a little old lady in the street. She was clutching her walking stick as if it were a human being. I don't want to be with you anymore, I don't want to get like her. Good-bye."

I didn't believe a word she said.

Song
Number 7

Hagen fetched Clara from the Financial Times building, where the *Diario* had rented a small office for her, and they drove silently into town. She had greeted him only with a nod. Later she laid her head on his shoulder, then leaned back again and looked out the side window. The time was five in the afternoon, but outside it was as dark as in the middle of the night. When they turned into Friedrichstrasse, Hagen put some music on, and the red and orange lights of the other cars danced in Cuban six/four time. That improved Clara's mood. Then it occurred to her that he had been listening to the same CD ever since she had known him. He had never moved the furniture around in his room either, as she did every three months, he always ate lunch at twelve-thirty, and when they went to the cinema he didn't want to discuss the movie afterward.

"What shall we eat?" said Hagen.

"I thought," said Clara, "I'd make a Mexican omelette and salad."

"That sounds good," he said.

"Or I could cook mole chicken and rice."

"Sounds good too."

"Or no, I don't want to cook."

"Are you tired?" he said.

"Yes."

They parked farther up, outside the Bang & Olufsen store, but didn't get out of the car. Hagen switched off the engine and the music and waited. Clara sighed. "You don't want to?" he said.

"No."

"Come on, then let's go on."

"No." She gave a forced smile. "Come on, *cuate*, let's go plunder the Galeries Lafayette."

Outside Günter was walking by. Or not walking, skipping along. His arms twitched, and if you didn't know him you'd think he was crazy. He was wearing his fur parka and under it one of the tight, shiny suits he wore to the office. His white face with its many burn scars and slanting eyes behind his rimless glasses was desperately beautiful.

Clara watched him go. Hagen had seen Günter too, and he noticed Clara watching him, but she didn't notice that he noticed. Hagen opened the door. The cold and the noise in the streets came into the car. He closed the door again, and the calm was quiet and comfortable once more.

"Like me to put some music on again?" asked Hagen.

Clara looked out the window. The glass was getting more and more steamed up. She could see only the outlines of passersby and the bright display window of the Bang & Olufsen store. They had been inside it a few times, but Hagen would never buy anything there. He thought it was too expensive. All the same, he never stopped talking about it.

"What did you say?" said Clara.

"Do you want to listen to music?"

"Yes, maybe."

He switched the CD player on, and after a few bars Clara said, "Turn it off, please."

He turned the music off again.

"Hagen," she said, "do you have just that one CD?"

"Why?"

"Ever since we've known each other, you've listened to nothing but that CD."

"It's La Lupe," he said. "You like it too, don't you?"

"Do you listen to it because of me?"

"What, me?"

"Yes, you."

"I have some more at home."

"I see."

One of the passersby was acting oddly. Instead of walking on like all the others, he stopped and quickly approached their car. The thin figure grew larger and larger, then only its face was visible outside the window. It must be a face, but Clara couldn't make much out through the clouded pane.

"Look at that," she said to Hagen, grinning.

Hagen smiled, a pained smile, and she suddenly understood and turned serious too. She stopped looking to the left and right. She hoped Günter would go on again as quickly as possible.

"Has he gone?" said Clara after a while.

"No," said Hagen, "he's still there. He's on my side now."

Clara wondered what she would do in Hagen's place. A Mexican man would have jumped out of the car long ago to chase the other man away. Hagen wasn't a coward—so why didn't he do that? He sat there, just like her, waiting. Perhaps he was afraid after all. Everyone knew Günter's story. Everyone knew who his father was, everyone had seen the photos and TV shots of his arrest thirty years ago, his naked, sinewy body tied to a stretcher, invulnerable as the body of San Sebastian. A man with a father like that need fear no one and nothing.

Günter alternately tapped the pane and put his face close

to it. He was only a few centimeters from them, but he didn't see them and they didn't see him. Clara sighed, then sighed again, then leaned quickly forward and wiped the condensation off the window on Hagen's side with her hand. But at that moment Günter turned and walked on, and from behind they saw only the pale fur rim of his hood bobbing up and down among the other pedestrians. She sat up straight again, perhaps a little too straight, and sighed.

She had always called Günter at the office when she couldn't bear it without him. He sat alone all day at his big glass desk in the Chancellor's office and had time to phone. They had phoned a great deal. Sometimes she called, sometimes he did, and either they talked about something or one of them said, I just wanted to give you a quick call, and an hour later they called each other again. Hagen almost never called. When he did, he had a reason. Once he had called just for the sake of it, but she didn't have time to talk, and since then he had never done it again. She never called him either.

"We can order something from the Thai place," Hagen said.

"Yes," she said.

"Shall we do that?"

"Yes."

"Are you sure?"

"Why wouldn't I be sure?"

"Right." He started the engine. "We'll order something from the Thai place."

"Hagen," she said.

He turned the engine off again. "Shall we go shopping after all?" he said.

She did not reply.

"You can tell me how to do it," he said.

"If we have eggs it's not difficult," she said.

"Eggs the way you cook them back home?"

"Yes, the way we cook them back home."

"Okay. I'll go, you wait in the car."

She said nothing again, and he said nothing, and then he said, "Red, green, and white—right?"

"Yes," she said.

"And which is what?"

"The tomatoes are red, the chillies are green, the onions are white."

"Yes," he said, "*claro.*"

Without a word she opened the door and got out. He jumped out of the car, but as soon as he was outside she sat down in it again. He sat down in the car too, and took her hand. He always touched her as cautiously as if it were the first time, and he did that now too, and he slept with her in just the same way.

"My father had a heart attack last night," she said.

He let go of her hand. "I'm sorry," he said.

"Yes."

"You didn't tell me."

"No."

"Are you going home?"

"No."

He took her hand again, and touched her fingers with his as apprehensively as if he hadn't done it a thousand times before.

"Hagen," she said.

"Yes."

"Could you hold me properly for once? Just for once . . ."

"Yes," he said. He clasped her fingers tightly, she shook her head, dissatisfied, and he pressed them even harder.

"Ouch, that hurts!"

"I'm sorry, Clara."

She closed her eyes and said nothing. She saw a huge yellow plate, one like they had at home, but much bigger. A tortilla lay on the plate, and her father was wrapped up in a linen cloth inside the tortilla; he was naked, with coins on his closed eyes. "Papa," she said quietly. "Yes, my angel," he quietly replied. He opened his eyes, and the coins fell to the floor. "Where are my colored stones?" she said. "The stones from Yaxchilán?" "Yes, those." "You took them to Germany with you." "No." "Yes, you did." "Are you sure?" "Quite sure, Clara. They were in your case, and we said, You're crazy, they're too heavy. But you said no, it didn't matter." "Yes—but where are they now? I don't know where they are. I just don't know!" "Have you really looked for them properly?" "Yes, last night, right after Mama called." "And did you look in your case too?" "No." "Go and look." "All right, Papa." "You

do that. And now leave me, I have to rest." "Wait a minute."
"No." He closed his eyes, and as if in a film running backward
the coins flew up from the floor and landed on his eyelids.
Although they were his eyelids, she felt the cold, heavy metal
on her own eyes. They were so heavy that she thought she'd
never be able to open her eyes again, but then she did, and
she saw that they were driving along the highway.

"Where are we going?" she said.

"Home," said Hagen.

"But we were going shopping."

"Clara," he said sternly, "you're not well."

"Say that again—just like that."

"Like how?"

"Well, just like that."

He didn't reply. He didn't look at her, and he did not take
her hand. He held the steering wheel and looked straight
ahead, and she thought, I wish he'd always hold me the way
he holds the wheel.

"You must always hold me like that," she said, and leaned
her head against his shoulder. She looked ahead with him
at the cars in front of them. Their rear lights shone in the
darkness almost as brightly as the stones from Yaxchilán. She
rubbed her head against his shoulder like a cat, he moved his
body slightly back but that was all the same to her, and after a
while he came closer again.

"I'll put music on, all right?" she said.

They were driving up Veteranenstrasse.

"Are you at all hungry?" he said.

"Not now," she said, "but I'm sure I will be later."

She pressed the skip forward button until 7 came up, because song number 7 was always the best on all CDs. It was a bolero, and if it hadn't been sung by La Lupe it wouldn't have been anything special. She had heard this bolero a thousand times before, and she would hear it a thousand times again. It was like life—everything stayed the same and didn't change, and if you were lucky it was good all the same.

"*Agua que no has de beber,*" sang La Lupe to ten thousand sighing, applauding people in the Estadio Azteca, "*déjala correr . . .*"

"*Agua que no has de beber,*" Clara sang along softly, "*déjala correr, correr, correr.*"

In Bed with
Sheikh Yassin

One fine, warm spring day ten years ago, a young bride was sitting alone in a hotel room in Tel Aviv. She sat on the bathroom floor in her pretty, new underwear, staring at the wedding dress hanging on the bathroom door, and then she stood up, took it off its hanger, and stuffed it into the laundry basket. After that she took her pretty, new shoes, went out on the balcony, and threw them off it. She liked the shoes, she had bought them at Henry's in Frankfurt with her grandmother, but now they dropped eight floors down, and one landed in the swimming pool. The other fell on the paving stones beside the pool; its sturdy white heel broke off and flew past the head of a small blond boy to land in the swimming pool as well.

She stood on the balcony looking down, but luckily the people below hadn't noticed what she had done, and no one happened to look up. She went in again, sat on the bed, and slowly lay down on her side. The light spring wind stroked her neck and her back, and she fell asleep at once. She had already dreamed of half her life when she was woken by a knocking at the door. It was more of a scratching than a knocking really, and a husky male voice said, "I'm going down, Esther." Then the voice said, rather more quietly, "Are you happy?"

"Yes," she replied, "very."

She opened her eyes and stared at the crumpled corner of the pillow right in front of her left eye, and she thought of the man out there. He was tall, he had long, slender fingers and a grave, doglike face. It was a face you could trust, but she'd probably thought so only because he was a doctor. Now she didn't think so anymore. Because she knew all about it now, about his trip to Cuba—"a farewell trip" he and his friends had called it—about Anna-Gabriela or Anna-Maria or what-ever her name was, the young English teacher from Santa Clara who let her apartment to foreigners, about the silly acci-dent they'd had during sex, about his childish terror. The idiot had told her mother, of all people, and she had told everyone else except her, and then only yesterday, by which time just about everyone in Frankfurt and Tel Aviv already knew about it, her mother had told her too. "Darling," she had said to her after the kiddush ritual down in the Leo Liebman Hall, "darling, there's something I have to tell you before anyone else does. But don't you worry, I'll do any worrying." And after she had told her about Cuba and Anna-Gabriela or Anna-Maria or whatever her name was, and about the Cuban condom that let them down, and David's childish terror, she said, "He loves you. He's sorry. If the two of you don't marry, that won't change anything now. Poor boy, he's been crazy with fear for weeks."

Poor boy. Sometimes she had the feeling that her mother was fonder of him than of her. Yes, she was certainly fonder of him than her. She had fished for him and she'd caught him. So now she added, "Nothing can have happened to him in that split second, Estilein, I mean, he noticed at once." And what about her? Poor boy, he'd been sleeping with Estilein for weeks, and killing her every time. Every time they were together he killed Estilein. Or at least he must have assumed that's what he was doing—and so did Mama!

"Darling, I'll just look in on Grandma in her room. Take your time. You have to be the most beautiful bride ever."

She raised her head from the pillow. "Yes, Mama," she called back. Then she let her head drop again.

Why didn't Mama catch it? she thought. Or why didn't someone like Sharon catch it? Or Sheikh Yassin. She hated Sheikh Yassin more than anyone in the world. She hated his small, feeble body, his long, girlish head that was always swathed in cloths, the reedy voice in which he wished death on people who weren't cripples like him. If there weren't any Jews around, he'd have some kind of objection to healthy Arabs.

They'd make a great pair, Sheikh Yassin and her, she thought, him mortally sick, and perhaps she was too. She was surprised to be thinking that, to be thinking that of all things, but you could think anything you liked even if it didn't make sense. You could imagine talking earthworms, or red oceans, or edible telephones, and now she was thinking what it would be like if she and the sheikh were in bed together. She wondered whether his head would still be wrapped in all those cloths, and whether he was as small and feeble down there as everywhere else. Then there was another knock on the door. She did not reply, and whoever had knocked said nothing and went away.

Dear God, she thought, what am I to do? I didn't make a mistake. He made a mistake, and now he's down there waiting for me, and all the others are waiting for me too, and I'm lying around here dreaming of Sheikh Yassin. Do I go down? Or do I lie here a bit longer? Please let me lie here a bit longer. I promise you I won't think of the sheikh anymore, or anything else pointless. I'll think about David and me, about our life and the family we could have. Please let me lie here a little longer, just a few minutes, maybe half an hour at the most.

80 Centimeters
of Bad Temper

They had met in Cracow, in Café Rim. Now they were sitting in Café Evropa in Ljubljana which, unfortunately, was a mistake. The rain drew little lines on the tall windows of the café; it was the middle of the day, but most of the cars had their headlights on. Looking through the glass door you could see to the end of Slovenská Boulevard, where the white hills of the Julian Alps were still resting after all their efforts in the last ice age. It was gloomy and dark outside, and inside too.

"Do you really have to go?" asked the young woman. She

had fair hair, dark eyes, and the cautious smile of a woman around thirty years old.

"Yes," said the man. He was ten years older, and that, she had thought from the first, was exactly the right age difference.

"Why don't we go to Dubrovnik?" she said. "It's still hot there."

"This is nothing to do with you."

"Or Rovinj. Rovinj is a beautiful place."

"It really isn't anything to do with you."

"No?"

"No. It's just this feeling, as if I were slowly breaking up from inside."

"A lot of people feel the same here at this time of year."

"Do they really?"

"You should be glad the mist isn't here yet. Everyone wants to go away when the mist comes down."

"I'll be glad to be home again," he said.

"It's because of me," she said.

"No," he said, "you're wonderful."

The sky above Slovenská Boulevard grew even darker, but a strip of light appeared beyond the mountains. Perhaps I ought to wait until the sky is blue again, he thought, perhaps this feeling will go away then. He stood up and said, "I'm going over there now. Will you wait?"

She looked gravely at him and took his hand. She held it tightly as if she would never let go, but when he withdrew it there was no difficulty.

"Maybe I won't get a flight now," he said. "God, I feel sick."

"Me too," she said.

He went out into the rain, and after a few steps took shelter in the entrance of a building. His legs were as heavy as if he'd been walking all day, and in addition it was raining even harder than before. Luckily it was only a few hundred meters to the travel agency. He could see the bright-yellow Lufthansa sign from where he stood, and suddenly he felt as if he were almost back home in Berlin. "Just a few steps," he said out loud to himself.

It was only a couple of minutes to get back to the café. He hurried in, ordered another espresso from the gigantic, taciturn waiter in passing, and dropped on the banquette with a sigh of relief.

"Done it," he said.

"When?" she said.

"Tomorrow morning."

"Then you can go straight to the doctor in the afternoon," she said.

"Doctor? Why would I need a doctor?"

"For your depression."

"Oh, yes. I see."

She clutched her glass of water until her knuckles were white. The glass broke, and it was a miracle that she didn't hurt herself.

"Tell him about me too," she said, standing up. "Oh, you won't anyway."

"I will if you want me to."

"What do *you* want, Itai?"

She turned and almost collided with the waiter. The waiter slowly put down the tray with the espresso and a glass of water and began carefully collecting the splinters of broken glass from the table. She said something in Slovenian, he smiled, she smiled too, and then she simply walked away. She stopped before opening the big glazed door and stood there for a few seconds. She went down Slovenská Boulevard, and only when she reached the black '30s tower block with the dried-up palm trees at the entrance did he lose sight of her. It wasn't raining anymore, but the wind sent scraps of paper and twigs blowing over the sidewalk.

It had all been so easy in Cracow. Well, not entirely. The stout Jewish young man from Microsoft whom she had visited there was in love with her, but she didn't feel the same about him. She was in love with Itai, but he didn't feel the same about her. He knew that he was not in love with her, but she didn't know it, so she'd said come and see me in Ljubljana sometime soon, it will be lovely. It will be lovely, he thought ten times a day before he set off. When he saw her in Ljubljana at the airport he thought, No, it won't.

They took a taxi into the city, she showed him the castle, the river, the bridges, it was all as pretty as in Cracow, only much smaller and less serious, and it rained without stopping. Then they went to her place, and she showed him her bed. She had only that one bed, which was eighty centimeters wide, and when he saw it he realized that he had been feeling sick all this time. Nonetheless, he slept with her in that bed. He lay awake in the night, his eyes kept opening again, and in the morning he told her he was a depressive. "That doesn't bother me," she said, and kissed him on the mouth. "But it bothers me," he said, "I have to go back to Berlin at once."

That had been this morning just after seven. Now it was two in the afternoon, and he still had sixteen hours of Ljubljana ahead of him. He took the travel guide out of his jacket pocket and began reading it. Baroque, Plečnik, Ljubljanica; a hundred and twenty days of mist a year. Somewhere there was a statue of the poet Prešeren who had hated his wife, with his half-naked Muse behind him pointing to where his mistress Julija lived. The market halls were very beautiful too, apparently. You could sit down by the water eating fried anchovies and looking at the pink Franciscan church. Or at Prešeren and his Muse. I'd look at the Muse, he thought. And then he felt: I feel so sick again.

"Are you feeling better?"

He looked up. There she was, back. Her hair was tousled, she had little drops of sweat or rain on her nose and her forehead, and she drew the corners of her mouth up into a smile that wasn't a smile.

"Yes," he said.

"May I?" she said.

"Yes—of course."

She sat down beside him and took his hand. She held it tight and passed her thumb over his, back and forth, back and forth, and he thought, Another fifteen hours, fifty minutes.

He had been like this even as a child. When he didn't want to do something he felt sick. Or that dreadful sense of heaviness came over him. Or both. The first week in a summer camp was always a catastrophe. His piano lessons. That one month with his father when Mama had the operation on her gallbladder.

"Do you like fried anchovies?" she said.

"Yes," he said.

"We could go and eat fish."

"Yes, why not?"

They sat there for a little longer, the waiter came, and she paid. The waiter went away, but they still did not get to their feet, and both of them stared at the big glazed door. It was still dark in the café, but how could it ever be light in here? The chairs had brown cord upholstery, the dusty lampshades hung much too low over the tables, and there was a very large black grand piano in the middle of the room. Beyond the glazed door the weather was slowly improving. The bright sunlit strip above the Alps almost filled the doorway, the sun reached Slovenská Boulevard, the cars were driving without their lights on.

"Come on," he said, "let's go into the city, we don't have much time left."

"*You* don't have much time left," she said, but he didn't hear her.

He quickly rose to his feet and went to the doorway, and he thought how he had been sitting in the train from Cracow to Berlin three weeks ago—sitting in his compartment, leaning his head against the cool windowpane with relief, and swearing never to go away again, because he hated being away from home. Then, when he arrived in Berlin, he was suddenly sad, even at the station, not to be in Cracow anymore. He would certainly miss Ljubljana too, he thought now, as he stepped out onto the slowly drying sidewalk, but not the woman he had visited there.

We Were Sitting
in Cibo Matto

This is the story I heard from my friend Alexis yesterday:

Alexis was at a party. He drank not too much and not too little, his arms and legs felt good, and he was smiling most of the time. When there weren't so many people in the Sam Club under the Jannowitz Bridge, he spotted Luisa. Her name isn't really Luisa, he said, and Fee, who would be in the story too, isn't really called Fee, but he had to be careful with the names.

Alexis had spoken to Luisa two weeks earlier at a reading at Pro qm, without really listening to what she said, and they had left together later. What Alexis liked most about Luisa was her thick, seventies-style brown hair. Apart from that he didn't say anything about her appearance. He just talked about her hair, and said he had kissed it a lot that first night. When he saw her again in the Sam Club he immediately wanted to bury his face in Luisa's warm locks again.

Luisa was dancing with Fee when Alexis noticed her. Later Luisa danced with Alexis, then with Fee again, and she kissed Fee as they danced. Then Alexis danced with Fee, then with Luisa, and now Luisa kissed him. During the next number Alexis and Fee kissed, and suddenly there was Luisa with them, she put one arm around Alexis, one arm around Fee, and kissed now him and now her. After that they danced again.

At this point Alexis told me he must stop for a moment, he'd be right back. We were sitting at the back of Cibo Matto, by the long wall, but not the wall with the large brightly colored picture, because we never sit there, but at the corner table opposite. He took his cell phone with him, and I saw him walking up and down in the street, talking on the phone. When he came back he said, "Johanna." He said no more. He just said "Johanna," and as Johanna is his wife's name I knew roughly how his story would go on.

The three of them left the Sam Club and went to Fee's place in Novalisstrasse. Alexis smiled as he said that. It was a surprised, proud, anxious smile, and he said he'd felt good at Fee's place right away. She had a great many books, blue linoleum, Bauhaus photographs above the desk, they might even have been the real thing. At Luisa's place, he said, he hadn't felt so good. Luisa was much younger than Fee, she had a room in a dark apartment in Greifswalder Strasse, and there were clothes, cigarette papers, pages torn out of ring binders, and checks lying around everywhere. Yes, Luisa was prettier than Fee, but she didn't really have a better figure, and he didn't find her quite so interesting.

"Okay, so then?" I said.

"Have you ever done it yourself?" he said.

"No," I said.

"*Oi, gamoto,*" he said, "you wouldn't believe it."

"So?"

"All night long."

He was smiling—triumphantly now. I smiled too, but I didn't like my smile. I didn't like it because I didn't like Alexis just now, but all the same I was smiling.

"Go on," I said.

He shrugged his shoulders. His phone rang. He went out, and when he came back he said, "Fee." Then he went on with his story. He said he had kept his eyes open most of the time, and when he closed them he had seen a huge, wide, pinkish gray sky such as he had never seen before. Ever since then he'd been obsessed by that sky, he had to see it again as often as possible.

Alexis is Greek, that's why he talks like that. But Alexis can be tough too. I don't know where he gets that toughness, maybe it's his character, maybe it has something to do with the fact that he was brought up by his grandparents as a child.

And perhaps he's tough only when he's talking about women or he happens to be drinking. And then there's his face: a little too broad, very intelligent, with black, angry eyes that look in slightly different directions.

"Well, first with one, then with the other," said Alexis after I'd asked how you go about it.

"And how does it end? I mean, the other one's feelings must be hurt."

"*Ts,*" he said, and for a second I smelled the aroma of roasted pistachio nuts, Santé cigarettes, and seawater. "I didn't come, of course."

"I see."

"Yeah."

I quickly finished my wine.

"A madhouse," he said.

"A madhouse?"

"Yes. Everyone doing it with everyone else. But I'll do it again. I never knew anything like it before."

We paid and left. Alexis phoned again, then I phoned. Then he phoned once more, and as he did I was thinking, The way he's been feeling for weeks is the way I feel when I've finished a novel. I'm on a high—and I know I'll soon start going down and down.

We decided to go to the Sam Club. We went along Weinmeisterstrasse to Alexanderplatz, and from there up horrible Alexanderstrasse to the Jannowitz Bridge. But this evening it wasn't quite so horrible, because of the Christmas market.

They'd put up more stands and rides than last year, there was a bigger Ferris wheel, a bigger roller coaster, and that tall steel pillar—people drop from it to the depths below with a jolt. The sky was full of bright red and blue lights, and where there were no lights it was infinitely wide and pinkish gray.

While Alexis went on talking I looked past him and up. Now he was talking about Johanna, his wife. Maybe she did know something, but she wasn't showing it. He spoke of her the way you speak of something you've had a long time. He didn't describe her. He didn't say what she said. Nor did he say what he said to her. She was just there—and maybe soon she wouldn't be there anymore.

"*Malakas*," he said suddenly, "you've no idea."

I looked past him again at the clear, wide night sky. Then I put my cap on, because it was getting cold. "No," I said, "I probably don't."

He put his own cap on too. It was one of those new, brightly colored bobble hats from Y-3 in which everyone looks like a man who would like to be a boy again, although he never was a boy. I'd bought one too, but luckily I lost it after three days.

"What are you thinking at this moment?" he said.

"What?"

"I asked what you're thinking at this moment . . ."

"Are you gay or what?" I said.

We laughed.

"I'm thinking . . . oh, you know what I'm thinking."

"No, not exactly."

"I'm thinking you'll have to stop soon."

"You're envious, admit it."

"Yes, there's that too."

We were standing at the big intersection outside the Jannowitz Bridge. The lights turned green, but we didn't walk. When they turned red we took a step forward at the same time, and stopped again at once. The junction was immersed in the gloomy, greenish light of East Berlin street lighting. The sky above it was still the way Alexis liked it.

"Look up," I said.

Alexis looked up. He didn't realize what I meant at once, but then he did. He looked gravely at me with his black, slightly squinting eyes, the lights changed to green, and we crossed the road.

We parted outside the Sam Club. I didn't want to go in with him. While I was waiting for a taxi to come along I turned to look at Alexis a couple of times. He was standing outside with the doorman, people were going past them, and whenever the door opened, a wave of bass music rolled out into the night. Then Alexis was suddenly gone. I just saw his blue and orange bobble hat disappearing through the open door among other people, the door closed, and it was quiet again outside for a few moments.

At last a taxi came. I got in and closed my eyes. "Number Six Veteranenstrasse," I said. "As quickly as possible, please." I felt very cold.

Melody

When Thomas and Melody fell in love, Iva had been dead for only two months. Melody called Meryll-Johnson in Chicago at once and said she wouldn't be coming back from her vacation in Europe, then they drove to Paris and took an apartment in the rue Céline. The moving company brought Thomas the rest of his things from Florence; Iva's parents had already collected her belongings and her furniture back in February.

In the winter Thomas decided to convert. Melody's parents found him a rabbi in East Hampton, but Thomas began putting the thing off. He was writing again now, and so long as he wasn't thinking of Iva as he wrote, it all went fine. Once, he told

Melody, in the middle of an argument, it had been too quick with them, to which she said: then go more slowly. And she slapped his face.

Thomas had himself circumcised in Mount Sinai on the Upper East Side. When he came to from the anesthetic he told Melody she must never go away again, and called her Iva. Three months later they married and moved to New York.

In New York, Thomas worked even less than he had after Iva's death. Mostly he lay in bed watching TV. Or he sat in the Columbus deli, looked out the window, and tried not to cry. Every other young woman who passed in the street reminded him of Iva. Then one day Iva sat down beside him. Her name was Andrea, her perfume was Dune by Dior, like Iva's, and also like Iva she had been to the Bettina School in Frankfurt. As they talked she sometimes laid her hand on his, sometimes they looked at each other in silence for a long time. All the same, they didn't exchange telephone numbers when they parted.

A year later, when Melody said she had fallen back in love with Abe, her first boyfriend, Thomas stopped speaking. Melody went on going to the company offices every day, Thomas wrote less than ever and didn't even go out. They sat together in front of the TV set, and Thomas alternately scribbled terms of abuse and endearments on a notepad and pushed it over to Melody. After a while neither of them could stand that anymore, and Thomas began speaking again. His first words were, "I'm going back to Germany."

And so it went on. Thomas met Andrea again in Frankfurt, walking down the street, and they had a son. Melody got pregnant by Abe, but lost the child when she heard that Abe's wife was pregnant too. Andrea didn't want to have little Ze'ev circumcised, and broke it off with Thomas. Thomas went to the West End Synagogue more and more frequently, he wasn't writing at all anymore, and he felt as if he were living inside a large, lilac-colored cloud of vapor. Melody contracted Klapisch syndrome, but made a miraculous recovery. Abe left his wife and child and sang "I Want to Hold Your Hand" outside Melody's window three nights running. On the fourth night Melody would have let him in—but on the way to see her he drove into the East River. Thomas met Judita at Simchat Torah in the synagogue, her perfume was Marc Jacobs, like Melody's, and she had been to the Bettina School, and they spent a few good months together. Then, six years later, Melody and Thomas sat together at the same table at a wedding in Tel Aviv. They had sex that night in Melody's room at the Hilton, and after that Thomas locked himself in the bathroom because he had to think about Iva and cry.

Thomas and Melody are now living together in the rue Céline again. They're doing fine.

The Right Time
of the Month

"Please," I said. "Let's do it one last time."

We were sitting in the Einstein, at the front with the tourists where we never usually sat, and I had to be back at the Charité hospital in twelve minutes.

"No," she said, "let's not."

"Do you really mean that?" I said. "Why not?"

"You're crazy," she said, and laughed. "You're the greatest nudnik I know."

We often laughed, even when there wasn't anything to laugh

about. I'd always thought that was a good sign, and perhaps it was the only reason why it had taken her so long to leave me.

She shook her head. "How can you seriously want to?" she said. She sounded hard, uncaring, Israeli.

"I've no idea."

"But it's over, Misha." That was a little gentler again.

"Well, that's why," I said.

At the moment I didn't even really want to—but what was I to do? I'd already tried everything else, and I couldn't think up anything new. The idea had come to me after consulting hours a few days ago. My last patient had been Samira. She was doing very well, she'd brought her daughter along and she was doing well too, and although Samira hated the little girl's father like poison, I suddenly thought, That might be the way to make it work.

After Samira had left, I stayed sitting there for some time. I didn't like the consulting room, they'd furnished it before my time, and they must really have thought that the dark-blue fitted carpet with little yellow and red stars on it, Mark Rothko prints, and a chunk of plastic rock crystal illuminated from inside would put women in a good mood. I sat at the desk, I rubbed the palms of my hands together, and thought about my plan. It could work that way, I kept thinking, I just have to pick the right time of the month, it has to be the right time of the month. Then I stood up and opened the window. Out in the garden the patients were going for a walk in the sun, and for the first time this year they weren't wearing winter jackets.

I laid my hand on Shelly's. She did not withdraw it, but her fingers were cold, and they were never cold usually. The waitress came and asked in a friendly way if we'd like anything else, and I was sure she had a Polish accent. Shelly didn't want anything more, and neither did I. All the same, I ordered another coffee.

"You have to go back," said Shelly.

I cancelled the coffee order. "This evening," I said. "I'm on duty until seven, then I'll come around to your place, we'll do it, and after that I'll go away at once."

"You're crazy," she said, "you're totally crazy."

"Oh, come on," I said, "don't be like that, not now."

"Stop it."

"You really won't do it? Why not?"

I pressed her hand, which wasn't so cold anymore. Shelly slotted her fingers through mine, our knuckles were jammed close, side by side, and it hurt quite a bit.

"Darling," I said.

I leaned over the table and kissed her on the mouth in front of everyone. Recently she'd almost never been kissing me back, and she didn't now, but suddenly, as I was about to stop, she did go on kissing me after all. Then she quickly turned her head away and looked down.

"How, then?" she said, still without looking at me.

"What do you mean?"

"How would we do it?"

I considered the question. "You up against the wall?" I said slowly.

"Yes, me up against the wall."

"For a long time?"

"Why not?"

"Then you on top of me?"

"Why not?"

"With your face to me?"

"Not at first. Then yes."

"And then we'd put our arms around each other?"

"Then we'd put our arms around each other."

"And hold each other tight?"

"Yes, tight."

"And then . . ."

"Then," she said, looking at me again, and she laughed, "then you'd have to be careful. You know that."

"Yes," I said to her, lying, "I know that. Of course."

Samira had been held prisoner for almost two months in the gym of her school in Plitvice. She had had a mattress, a blanket, a few books from the school library, there was something to eat twice a day, always at different times, usually bread, tomatoes, and crackers. The women and girls in the gym were taken away by different men each time, often by two or three militiamen at once. Only one of them was interested in Samira, and that was Zelko, once a fellow pupil of hers and the son of her class teacher. Mrs. Galic had disappeared two months back, when the mujahedin were still in charge, and after that the Serbs took over, Zelko among them.

Zelko took Samira home with him, to his mother's deserted, untidy apartment. They sat in silence for a long time in the kitchen, eating canned fish or frozen pizza, and Samira felt sick, although she'd been hungry for weeks. Then they went into Mrs. Galic's bedroom. When Zelko had finished Samira had to stay lying beside him, stroking his back, and he told her how they'd be happy together someday in New Zealand, where his two cousins lived. She said nothing, and he said he could understand that she needed time, he himself had known ever since the fifth grade that she was the girl for him, so he had a start on her there. Then he took her back to the gym, and stroked her sweaty hair back from her forehead when he said good-bye. As soon as he had gone she flung herself facedown on the mattress. She lay like that for hours without shedding a single tear.

It was some time before Samira told me all this. At first she sat facing me in our ridiculous consulting room as apathetically as she had cowered on her mattress in Plitvice. All the same, I was the one she always wanted to see, although most women preferred my female colleagues, and we talked about Berlin, books she liked, clothes she'd seen somewhere. One afternoon she asked me if I thought it would be uncivil of her. I asked her what she meant. She said if she told me something in confidence. No, I said, I'd think it uncivil of her if she didn't. I choked and began coughing. After that Samira told me how she got pregnant, how she wanted to abort the baby but didn't after all, and everything else.

"I'm going away soon," said Shelly coldly, almost angrily. It was her Israeli tone of voice again.

"Where to?" I said.

"Israel."

"For a long time?"

"I don't know."

"Will you find work there?"

"I don't know."

She withdrew her hand from mine, leaned back and looked past me. Her hair fell over her face, and she blew it aside like a teenager.

"Are you going alone?" I said.

"Don't ask that," she said. "Why do you ask that?"

"Because I want to know."

"Good."

"How do you mean—good?"

"Yes, I'm going alone."

"You are?"

"Yes. But he may follow me."

"I'm sure he'll follow you."

"Yes, I'm sure too."

"And he's sure to go and see the mohel for you."

I laughed. I know my laugh sounded artificial, but after all, it was.

"Stop it," she said.

"What?"

"Stop laughing, will you?"

"Will you stay there for good?"

"Maybe."

"With that *scheigetz*?" I sounded like my father when he was talking about one of his German customers.

"I'll only tell you that," she said, grinning, "if you stop grinning in that silly way, you little shtetl Jew."

"You're grinning too."

"Yes, but not in a silly way."

"That's true."

I reached for her hand again, but she drew it away.

"How am I going to live without your laugh?" I said. "Tell me that."

"And how am I going to live without yours?"

Time stood still, it turned once in a circle and came back again, much too fast. Shelly breathed deeply in and out, I breathed deeply in and out, and then I said, "At seven, right? Directly after work."

"Stop it," she said. "And do pay, you're going to be late."

She stood up and went to the ladies' room. She left her purse on the banquette. I watched her going and thought, Please, it must be the right time of the month! Then I called for the waitress, and while I was paying I asked, in Polish, if she was a Pole. No, she said in her friendly tone.

My idea was very simple, and normally it was women who did this kind of thing. I knew it would work, I just had to get Shelly to the point, the rest wouldn't be any problem. She was always the more unreasonable of the two of us, and I'd either act as if I had in fact been careful, or I wouldn't even do that, and afterward I'd just apologize profusely and pray it had worked.

"I'll think it over," said Shelly. She was standing behind me, stroking the back of my neck. Then she put her arms around me and kissed me on the same spot. "I'll call you later, you lunatic."

I helped her into her coat, and as we went out she took my arm. People were looking at us, we both noticed that, but they didn't notice that *we* noticed. People always looked at us. She pressed her arm close to me, and it was almost like before.

Outside it was still cold and wintry, but you could see the sky again, and we didn't fasten our coats. On Friedrichstrasse we said good-bye. Shelly was going back to the Institute, I had to take the tram. We didn't embrace, and we didn't kiss. We smiled at each other, then we parted.

Last time she was with him, Samira tried to kill her Zelko. He had simply fallen asleep while he was talking about New Zealand, and she went into the kitchen, picked up the knife that was still lying in the pizza carton, and came back with it. She knelt above him in the bed and swung back her arm, but then the knife fell from her hand, she herself didn't know if it was by chance or on purpose. The knife flew across the room and landed on the radiator with a clang, and Zelko woke up. He saw her above him and smiled, and said, "Oh, dear heart, how lovely to see you there. Come on, kiss me." And she kissed him, because she had no option.

Fearing
for Ilana

They had once sat down together. They had once all sat down together, and after that it looked as if Wladek would cause no more
problems.

Beforehand, Wladek had been saying those strange things all
the time; it was no use, he said, people couldn't do this to him.
He'd rather take her with him forever—but living alone, without
Ilana, was like being dead for him, he couldn't manage it. So
they met, he, Ilana, and Uri. A German girl who was a friend
of Ilana's was there too, and she talked to that idiot so sternly

that in the end Wladek said okay, okay, I understand. He added that it was his own unreasonable thoughts he hated so much, they were like a thousand little devils stabbing him to the heart with their pitchforks from inside, but now it didn't hurt him anymore, everything was okay, no one had to worry about him. As he left he hugged Uri and wished him and Ilana luck, which was totally crazy, because it was his own and Ilana's old apartment he was leaving, and why did he hug Uri anyway?

He had hugged him much too tight, as Uri realized only now. He had put his long, basketball player's arms around Uri's torso like twining plants, and squeezed so hard that Uri choked and uttered a funny, awkward, gurgling sound, but Ilana didn't hear it. Perhaps her German friend did. When they went to the police yesterday, she told Uri it had been obvious that their meeting with Wladek had achieved nothing. His eyes had been dull from the beginning to the end of it, like the eyes of someone who has just a single, blind idea in his head, and won't look at the world outside himself anymore. She had seen that very clearly, she said, anyone who wanted could have seen it. And that, for God's sake, was why Uri ought to have kept an eye on Ilana, he ought to have kept an eye on her day and night, and his late arrival at the 103 Club on Valentine's Day had been shit, such shit that no one could absolve him of the guilt. The way that German cow said it made Uri feel he was as much of an idiot as Wladek.

Now he was late again. So? That was the way he was, he couldn't help it; the Realtor he'd arranged to meet about the key to Ilana and Wladek's old apartment was waiting for him all the same. Ilana ought to have waited for him too, but she never did wait, she didn't wait on the evening of Valentine's Day either, she went off on her own, and then it happened. People always waited for him usually. Whenever they wanted something, and even when they didn't want something, they waited. Of course the Realtor, an old-fashioned and loquacious character from West Berlin, let nothing show, except that when he paid for his four beers he said, "Four beers in an hour—that's four too many." He was prancing about comically as he left, although he must have been over fifty, and in his gray flannel suit and well-worn Italian shoes he sat with the young people in the 103 looking like a battered old car.

Uri watched him go, glancing through the window he saw the old man get into his dark blue BMW, and he thought. On the evening of Valentine's Day, when she was to go with him to fetch the last of her things from the old apartment, she had been sitting at the window near the entrance as usual, so he would never sit there again, that was the least he could do. He had told her earlier on the phone that she mustn't on any account go to the old apartment without him, he definitely wouldn't be late, and if he was she was to wait, she absolutely must wait, but she didn't. As the waitresses told him, she must have left again after five minutes. She hadn't ordered anything to drink, she sat there leafing through a few newspapers, then she got up and went to the bar and left a message to tell him she had gone ahead, he must follow. She was terribly impatient, more impatient than usual, which was why the little bottle-blond Syrian girl who was serving asked why she was so impatient, and Ilana told her because whatever happened she didn't want to meet her ex-boyfriend in their old apartment. But then she did meet him there, he was standing behind the bathroom door, and he strangled her.

When Uri arrived in Christinenstrasse on the evening of Valentine's Day he had already guessed what had happened. The lights over the stairway were out of order, as usual, but up on the third floor where the apartment was, light fell on the stairs at an angle through the open door. He ran upstairs, and as he did he slipped, he only just managed to catch hold of the banisters at the last moment. If he hadn't, who knows how badly he would have fallen? All was still in the apartment. There were lights on in all the rooms, and the silence was so very silent because the apartment had been emptied, but then Uri heard a sound after all. He heard a slapping sound, a soft, regular slapping, and he followed that sound to the bathroom. First he saw him: Wladek standing there perfectly rigid, his face distorted in a grimace, and Wladek kept striking the back of his neck with the flat of his hand and muttering, "What about me? What about me? What about me?" Ilana was lying on the floor in front of him, she was lying beside the bathtub. She was longer than the bathtub, and Uri still remembered asking himself in that first moment: If she's longer than the bathtub how does she fit into it? Then he bent over her. He saw her purple face, her purple lips, there were hundreds of little red marks on her eyes, and her throat was striped red and white.

They had often been to the 103 Club together in the old days. They met for breakfast in the middle of the morning, when he was up and Ilana had already been at her desk for a few hours. They went there early in the evening, that was the time they liked best. Sometimes they sat there at night, they sat for hours on the seats in the window looking at the road junction and the trams, they would say, "One last cigarette and then we'll go! One last beer and then we'll go!" Those were often the best and longest evenings. They'd even met at the 103 Club. It was where they had their first quarrel, it was where they signed the contract for the new apartment in Kastanienallee, although they'd lived there together for only two weeks because that idiot had strangled Ilana in the old apartment—and at the very moment when that occurred to Uri his cell phone rang, and it was the Realtor saying the key doesn't fit, you gave me the wrong key. So he looked, and the Realtor was right. He was holding the Christinenstrasse key, the Realtor had the Kastanienallee key, and that was fine, that was absolutely fine, it meant that if he went home tonight he wouldn't be able to get in, and he didn't want to go home tonight at all. Without a word he ended the call and turned off his cell phone.

With Wladek, Ilana once told him, she always came at once. She hated him, at least she hated him at the end; she couldn't have hated him yet at the beginning. She hated that idiot so much, but as soon as he was inside her she came. "With me," said Uri, "you need much longer and sometimes you don't come at all. Why's that?" "Because I love you," said Ilana, and to this day he didn't know what she meant by that.

The Right of Young Men

It had been stormy for days. The sky was often so bright that it hurt to look up at it, and then it darkened again. The warm April wind drove garbage and broken twigs ahead of it. Sometimes you heard an open window nearby slam back against the frame with the sudden sound of breaking glass. Flights were constantly being delayed. Almost every night I was in a different hotel in a different city, and when I woke up in the morning I would cross that city off my list.

In Frankfurt I slept at my parents' place. I hadn't been there for a long time; after the trial I gave up my apartment at once and moved away. I had no problems with Frankfurt, but Frankfurt had problems with me, and although I'm quite self-confident I don't like being surrounded by people who'll always see me as the criminal who was acquitted.

I put my case down in the corridor, washed my face, and went to Café Laumer. I hoped to meet someone from the old days there, and then I'd see if anything had changed. But no one was there, and none of the older ones, who blamed me less—or so it had always seemed to me—than the younger ones, perhaps because they too had had to act in a similar way sometimes during the war. They never talked to us about that time, not to this day, and if they did they said nothing about what they'd done themselves. It was all about what had been done to *them*. My father was like that, they were all like that, only Miriam's father was more honest.

I left the money on the table, and when I was outside I realized I hadn't left enough, but I didn't go back. I went slowly along Bockenheimer Landstrasse to the Literaturhaus, and it was still too early. Suddenly it turned dark, I felt something catch me in the back and I staggered, then the wind fell again and the white, cold sun reappeared.

She was standing on the corner of Rothschildstrasse. She didn't see me, and when I saw her I turned at once and went back the way I had come. After a little while I turned again and went straight toward her. I looked her in the eye, and she looked back at me.

"Hello," I said.

"Ariel," she said.

"How are you?" I said, sounding stern without meaning to.

"How are *you*?"

She didn't look any older, but she seemed different all the same. I don't know what it was, probably grief, but if she had always had such an expression on her face then I hadn't noticed it. She looked more Jewish, in any case.

"I'm okay," I said. "Or no, I'm not."

"That's a pity."

"Yes, it is."

"I'm coming to the reading," she said.

"You are?"

"Don't you want me to?"

I wanted to take her hand, but she noticed, and took a step back. I took a step forward and held my hand out. She gave me her hand, our fingers touched, and I felt bad.

"Don't do that," she said, "or you'll make me cry."

I would have liked it if she'd cried. "Yes," I said, "sorry."

During the reading she sat where I couldn't see her. The story I read didn't go over particularly well. Or perhaps it did go over all right, I don't know exactly, I was thinking of something else while I read. After the reading I talked to someone for a little while, and Miriam stood somewhere waiting for me. Suddenly she was gone. I was relieved, and thought, Why did none of my old friends come except for her? The others were going to Isoletta, although I decided to go to her place and said good-bye.

She had lived alone since it happened. Her father owned an apartment building in the Nordend district, on the crossing of Baustrasse and Schwarzstrasse, where cars have to go slowly around a small, sharp bend and it's all a little like Florence. Although she could have the whole building for herself, she lived in the smallest apartment. I'd been there only once, just before I moved away. We had stood in the kitchen, I picked her up and put her down on top of the refrigerator, but then she thought of Eldad or something of that sort, and we stopped, and soon after that I left.

Now I was back. I rang, she immediately pressed the buzzer. She was standing upstairs in the doorway, looking very tall and very thin, her hand resting on the door handle.

"You read well," she said.

"Really?"

"Yes. You know I like to hear you read."

"I'd forgotten."

"I miss that."

"I miss you."

"I miss you too."

We sat down in the kitchen, but she didn't ask if I'd like anything to drink. The table was by the window, and as we talked we could see the trees outside rocking back and forth in the wind. The moon kept appearing between the black leaves and branches, and it all looked normal and uncaring.

"Do you have someone now?" she said.

"Do you?"

Neither of us replied.

"I don't think about such things," she said.

"You don't?"

"No. Do you?"

"Yes, I do."

"That's good."

"But not so much."

"You don't have to lie to me, I don't mind."

"I'm not lying."

"In a week's time," she said, "it will be exactly four years ago."

"You still remember the day?"

"Yes."

"I didn't want it to happen," I said.

"I know you didn't."

"Really?"

"It wasn't your fault. It was my fault, and his fault."

"But I did it."

"If you hadn't done it," she said, "he would have done it."

"Would you still have been with him, then?"

"Maybe."

"And now?"

"You mean now that he's dead?"

"Yes—now that he's dead."

"I'd have liked it better than before."

"And with me?"

"With you too."

I stood up so quickly that the chair tipped over backward, and I was only just in time to catch it. Everything was the way it used to be. That was better than nothing, but not good either. We'd tried too often to find an end or a beginning, and neither had worked, because Eldad never said no of his own accord. What she said, unfortunately, made no difference, because she would say something else the next day. Only when Eldad, gentle, cool-natured Eldad, took out his army pistol in my apartment did matters come to a head. No one knew how he had managed to bring that pistol back from Israel to Germany, but never mind, he brought it out, and from then on things couldn't go on the same as before.

"Don't you really have anyone?" she said.

"I do, yes," I lied.

"Is she beautiful?"

"I don't know."

"That's what you always say."

"Yes, I know."

"Is she clever?"

"Yes."

"Does she understand your jokes?"

"Yes. Well, most of the time."

"Is she like me?"

"Stop that."

"Is she like me?"

I looked down at the empty table.

"You can tell me, it's all right."

Back then I was sometimes so furious with her that I could have hit her. Of course I never did. Just sometimes, before we slept with each other, I pushed her arms down on the bed or put my hand around her neck. Then she got angry and sat on top of me and did something that hurt, I forget now just what it was.

"Will you stay the night here, Ariel?"

I stood in the kitchen doorway, looking at her in surprise, and I thought, Yes, yes, yes.

"No," I said.

"Okay," she said.

"Good night, Miriam."

"Good night."

Outside it was still windy and too warm. I looked down at the sidewalk as I went along, counting the gray stone slabs under my feet. I think it was sixty-three or sixty-five paving stones to Eschersheimer, exactly three hundred to Eysseneckstrasse. Outside the building where my parents lived I sat down on the park bench where I always used to sit as a little boy, when I didn't want to go home yet. The wind blew through my coat, the noise of cars in Miquelallee sounded louder than it used to be, and I wondered why my parents had to be in Bad Soden this week of all times. It was probably better that way. They were old people, and old people always know the best thing to do in such circumstances.

On the day after the trial I had met Miriam's father at Café Laumer. We hadn't arranged it beforehand, but I knew he knew I'd be there, and I knew he would too. We arrived at the same time and sat down at the last table in the garden. Even before we ordered he said, "You live your whole life with this kind of thing, Ariel, but you go on living."

"What about Miriam?"

"Miriam too."

"Will she?"

"Yes, she's been indulged, but she'll learn to live with it."

"She never wants to see me again, Herr Herschkowits."

"Give her time."

"How much time?"

"As much as she needs."

"Who gave you time back then?"

"I took the time myself, my boy, and then one day it was all right. I was even glad I'd done it."

"How many?"

"One in Pressburg, then two in Kosice. What happened up in the mountains never meant anything to me."

He put his hand on my arm and looked at me hard. He had a small, shrewd face, and with his thick gray hair he looked the image of an elderly Jew, but he could also have been an elderly German.

"Everything is what we make of it, Ariel," he said. He pressed my arm affectionately, stood up, and went to another table where his friends were sitting. They were all shrewd elderly people like him, and I wondered how many dead men they had to their collective account.

The wind blew through my coat one last time, the sleeves billowed out, my scarf almost flew away, and then, after all those stormy days, it was calm at last. The final gust of wind was like the tail of a huge black cat finally disappearing into the yard next door.

I stood up and took the key out of my trouser pocket. It was the key I always took out of my pocket as a child when I came home from school. Now I went up to the front door with the key, but then I put it back in my trouser pocket and turned around, and I thought: Nothing's simple, life in itself isn't simple, not even sudden happiness.

On a Cold, Dark Night

"You know something?" he said. "The most important thing about a woman is her skin."

"Oh, really?" she said.

"Yes," he said. "It can be soft or a little taut, and that's good. Sometimes it's stretched too tight, and you suspect that something's wrong."

She nodded.

He was wearing an expensive brown suit fitting closely over the shoulders and with narrow lapels, which looked good on him. He had cold, sad eyes, he was unshaven and tired.

"Of course the skin at the nape of the neck isn't the same as the skin on the arms or the belly—and it smells different everywhere. It smells like lemonade, like sea air, like a memory. You know, I can tell from a woman's skin how she's feeling at the moment."

"Really?" she said.

"Yes."

They were the last guests in the InterConti bar, she knew that, and they both felt a little awkward.

"So how am I feeling, then?" she asked.

He looked at her and thought, She looks younger than her real age, it's two in the morning and here she is sitting alone with me.

He placed one hand on her forearm, and stroked the fine blond hairs. Then he stopped stroking, propped his elbows on the bar counter, and ordered another beer for himself from the bartender, and one for her too.

"You're a brave woman," he said, "but sometimes too brave."

"So how am I feeling?"

Bad, he thought, and said, "When you're excited you get red blotches on your neck."

"Like now?"

"Yes," he lied.

"No," she said, "that's not so."

"I haven't been here for fourteen years," he said suddenly.

"Really? Where do you live?"

"In Tel Aviv."

"Tel Aviv?"

"Yes—in Tel Aviv. What are you thinking about?"

"Nothing," she said, "nothing at all. Why did you leave?"

"One of them had skin that suddenly felt as thick as leather—and the other one's skin was as delicate as if she were my daughter."

"And why are you here now?"

"Because of you."

"Lucky we didn't miss each other."

"You won't believe me anyway," he said, "but I was homesick. And when you're homesick you have to do something about it. I was homesick for trees that are really green, for Maredo and the Fressgasse, for white skin that flushes red when you kiss it too much."

"Why wouldn't I believe you?"

"Because you said 'Tel Aviv' in such a funny way just now."

"Tel Aviv," she said. "Is that better?"

"And you?" he said.

"Me?"

"Yes, you."

"What about me?" she said.

"Yes," he said, "what about you?"

"I thought you knew everything."

He ran his finger over her forearm again, then down her throat and along her bare collarbone.

"You've nearly had enough," he said. "You keep thinking about it, and you don't have an answer. Your friends don't ask you anymore. They say it's because of you, not the men. Why do you always pick the same kind of man, they've asked you, and at first you discussed it with them. They said those available are the only ones there are, that's what your friends don't understand. That's why you're alone with your problem. And now—I know this too—you'll stand up and leave, and we'll never meet again."

She took her glass and put it back on the counter without drinking from it.

"I must go to the ladies'," she said, "and maybe I won't come back."

She took a couple of steps, then turned and said, "Is my neck red?"

"Yes," he said.

"I know," she said.

A few minutes later he picked up his phone and tapped in a Frankfurt number.

"Jakow," he said quietly, "were you asleep? Jakow, Jakow, listen, I think it works. Yes, the asshole act works, and so does the Israel act. Just like you said, you genius! . . . In the InterConti, yes . . . Yes, I booked a room already. No, I'm hanging up now."

He ended the call, put the phone down without a sound,

and ran his fingers over the counter. The counter was cool and shiny, and he closed his eyes and imagined how it would be very soon upstairs. He'd ask her to undress first, then he'd look at her for a long time. He would look at her white, blond body, her white breasts, her white throat, her white thighs, her white face. Then they would kiss, they'd kiss for a long time, a very long time, and her face would turn red at once, and so would her throat and her belly. He would ruffle up her short blond hair, he would stroke her white skin all over and kiss her, perhaps hit her a bit if she'd let him, and at every touch of that white German skin she would sigh, every sigh would move him, and she would be very close to him and he to her. He smiled, opened his eyes again, and thought, This will be a good night for a change.

He waited another half hour and then asked for the check. As he put on his coat he wondered briefly whether to go and look for her in the ladies' room. He went to reception, paid for the room, and went home in a taxi. As they were going up Grüneburgweg it began to rain. The rain lashed against the black windowpane, the orange streetlights rushed by outside, someone was staggering around in front of the green, neon-lit window of the big sandwich bar, stumbled, and fell.

I must try it again as soon as possible, he thought, as soon as possible.

You're Greta

They met on the corner of Choriner Strasse and Schönhauser Allee, outside the magazine kiosk with the white shutters and green metal roof. There was also a girl there to make Greta up, and a thin, bearded young man from the magazine that Greta didn't know at all. Maarten had sent them both away quickly, and his little assistant, a Japanese or Korean girl, didn't stay long either.

It was four-thirty already, and in fact the appointment had been for one o'clock, but yet again she hadn't made it in time. At one p.m. she had only just set off from Hamburg, and when she looked at the time as she boarded the train at the Dammtor station she thought, I really ought to be there by now. She knew that Maarten wasn't just anyone, so she had been looking forward to today for weeks—but she wasn't just anyone either, and since so far people had always waited for her, she felt sure that he would wait too.

It had been one of those typical Greta mornings again. She was still asleep when Hanka took the little boy to school, and when she woke up the apartment was quiet and empty. She stood at the window in her pajamas for a long time, teacup in hand, looking at the Grindel tower blocks, she imagined the enormous number of people inside them, and the thought made her a little dizzy. Then she went into the bathroom, and in the bathroom she was still thinking of the people in the Grindel tower blocks. She thought of their apartments, their children, their beds, and she wondered how many of those many, many people had seen her in the cinema or on TV, and how many of them knew her name or had even said it out loud. That made her dizzy again, and suddenly she missed the little boy and decided to make sure she collected him from school today. But she didn't, because at Heymann's bookstore they had Maarten's Tokyo book ready for her, she was going to look through it on the train, but she didn't make it to the bookstore either. In the end she was glad to have caught the one o'clock Intercity-Express, because the next left two hours later, and she couldn't possibly travel on the ordinary Intercity.

Of course Maarten had waited. He had certainly not spent all that time standing outside the kiosk, which in the fading afternoon light looked delightfully old and East German, but when she got out of the taxi he was there beside her at once, and said in German, "Hello, I'm Maarten. You're Greta." You're Greta—the way that sounded! Then he said quietly it might be too dark already. At that moment it started raining, but they had to try all the same, and at first she was taken by surprise every time the flash lit up the old, black buildings around them with silver.

Maarten was clever, or cautious, or perhaps something quite different. He didn't tell her what to do, she didn't care much about that, but whenever she did something he pressed the shutter release. She didn't want to stop, although she was feeling so cold in her thin black dress. But then, she was always cold, even in summer, so that made no difference to her. She imagined how she would look in the pictures, tall, a little too thin, a soft and far too large, vulnerable mouth that always captivated everyone. She leaned against the pretty, old kiosk, the street gleamed in the December rain, and life was so beautiful, but sad too because it would end someday. Then she thought that she could buy a pretty picture book for Elias at the station, preferably one with a nice old magician in it, and she immediately felt better.

"Okay, thanks," Maarten said suddenly in a quiet voice. She smiled, and noticed that she was smiling, then she fetched her bag from his car and put her trench coat on over her dress in the middle of the street. The coat was made of black parachute silk, so they'd told her at Miyake's, but she didn't believe it.

Would she do that again without a dress under it? Maarten said.

"Put it on or take it off?" she said.

"Put it on, please," he said.

She went behind the kiosk and took the coat off, then her dress, put the coat on again, and came back and waited. Maarten looked in the camera, glanced up again, looked in the camera once more, then he put the cover on the lens and it was over.

After that they went to Paris Bar.

A few guests looked up as they came in, and she acted as if she didn't notice, but she felt a little dizzy. The proprietor said her name out loud, and looked curiously at Maarten. The whole thing lasted no more than two or three seconds. Luckily he gave them a place on the front banquette on the left, at one of the tables without tablecloths on them where some of the regulars usually sat. They sat down side by side on the cold leather of the banquette, and she kept turning to Maarten as they talked, but he looked past her out the window at Kantstrasse in the dark.

Maarten had short brown hair, but not really short, he had an attractive mouth, although again not as attractive as all that—and he was one of those men who look younger than they are and it shows. The man with whom she'd shared the *Kill Bill* disaster was one of them, and so was Elias's father, and she had no idea if she liked that or if she didn't. Sometimes yes, sometimes no. She'd liked it in Elias's father; with Mr. *Kill Bill* it quickly got on her nerves. They had gone to see that frightful movie together, so the whole thing ended before it could even begin. She had been doing yoga with Hanka beforehand, which always made her very sensitive, and suddenly there was all that blood and those flying, screaming Japanese, and Uma never looked anything but sad or vicious. After the movie she had to go home at once. She wanted to get away from the man who'd been sitting beside her in the cinema and didn't realize how she felt, who had failed to say, "Come on, let's go!" after half an hour of it. At home, after she had cleaned her teeth, she sat on the side of the bathtub with her toothbrush in her hand, staring at the brown watermark above the boiler.

"What's it like in London?" she said.

"Oh, fine," said Maarten.

"Really?"

"I've been there since 1983," he said, and you could hear his Dutch accent.

"Since 1983?" said Greta.

"Yes."

"That's a long time."

"Yes, a long time."

"Fine," she said.

"Hm," he said. "Yes."

She rose to her feet and smoothed her dress out, and she noticed that she was still cold. In the ladies' room she examined her mouth in the mirror as she phoned Bernhild about France. Bernhild was still at the agency, she sounded tired and bored, and they soon ended the call. Then she called the child, but Hanka said he was already in bed and she was just reading him a bedtime story, she'd better call back in the morning.

"I always seem to myself so ridiculous," she said when she was sitting next to him again.

"You do?" he said.

"Yes," she said.

"Why?"

"I'm too thin. And I hate my mouth."

"Okay."

"I hated it even as a child. Everyone said look, what a lovely big mouth little Greta has."

"Really, even as a child?"

"Yes. My son's mouth is the same."

"How old is your son?"

"Eight. No, nine. No, wait a minute . . . eight. Yes, eight."

"Shall we go?" he said.

"No," she said, "why?"

"I'd like to take a few more pictures."

"Where?"

"In the hotel."

"What kind of pictures?"

"Of the other Greta."

"The other Greta?"

"Yes."

"There isn't any other Greta."

"No?"

"No."

"Are you sure?"

"Yes."

They stayed quite a while longer in Paris Bar. She asked him what Diane Keaton was like, and Gwen Stefani, and Missy Elliott, but he didn't want to talk about them. He didn't want to say much about Tokyo either. In fact he didn't want to tell her anything, but all the same he didn't stand up to go. So she talked.

She told him about Elias's father, she and the little boy hadn't seen him for two years because he was in the Fuhlsbüttel penitentiary. She told him about the dark green waters of the Isebek Canal, where a drowned body had been found drifting every spring for as far back as she could remember. And she described the place on the bank, opposite Elias's school, where she sometimes stood in summer and watched the little boy playing with the other kids in the schoolyard at break. She said something about her mouth again, but by now it was getting on her own nerves, and she asked Maarten whether she ought to accept a small part in a French production, a part that was really much too small for her. Before he could reply she said, "Oh, never mind." After that she didn't say much anymore, they both looked out at dark Kantstrasse in silence, and later someone from *Bild am Sonntag* came over to their table, a nice, blond, stupid young man in a suit. She didn't know what he wanted, she could hardly hear him because she was feeling dizzy again, and as soon as he had gone she wasn't dizzy anymore, which was such a pleasant sensation that she had to laugh out loud, right out loud. As she did so, she looked into Maarten's eyes, which were attractive but not really attractive, and now he laughed too for the first time, and they paid and went over to the Savoy.

As they were crossing Kantstrasse, Greta thought of the Isebek Canal again. The black asphalt beneath their feet was dark, green, deep water, and she was the dead body drifting in it.

Butterflies

"There's a snake, a rose, and a tiger," he said softly.

"Anything else?" she said.

"Yes, a butterfly."

"The tiger," she said.

"Where?"

"In front, on my hip bone. You're always talking about it anyway."

She raised her skirt, put her hand between her legs, and turned to him. They were sitting at his desk, she on his chair, he on the piano bench, and the screen of the laptop, which had soft music coming out of it, shone pale blue. Otherwise it was dark in the room, only the small light beside the bed was still on.

"Will you kiss me?" he said.

"No."

"Why not?"

"Oh, shut up and do it!"

She offered him her hip, he placed the child's tattoo over the right place, and pressed it firmly down with the small blue towel that he had moistened beforehand in the bathroom.

"You mustn't move or it won't stay on," he said.

"Mustn't move for how long?"

"A long time."

He tried kissing her as he held the towel in place, but she pressed her lips together and turned her head aside.

"What's the idea?" he said angrily. He took the towel away, carefully removed the wet sheet of film, and a savage, dark-blue tiger was looking at him. Her skin was even whiter there than on the rest of her. Against the blue tiger it was milky white.

"Now what?" she said.

"The butterfly," he said.

"Where?"

"On your breasts."

"Right, on my breasts."

She unbuttoned her blouse, pushed her breasts up with her hands, and together they decided which breast would suit the butterfly best.

"You hold the towel there," he said. "I want to listen to something else."

He turned to the laptop, and Minnie Riperton came on instead of 50 Cent.

The butterfly had big, dark-red wings, and her breasts looked even larger and paler with it. She looked down at herself in surprise and smiled, then adjusted her blouse again and looked gravely at him. He returned her gaze. After a while she turned to face him fully, and propped her feet on the piano bench to the right and the left. Once again they studied each other in silence.

"Don't even think about it," she said.

"You're crazy," he said. He put a hand on her knee and slowly ran his fingers up the inside of her thigh.

"No," she said.

He withdrew his hand.

"I'm the woman, understand?" she said. "So stop being angry."

"Come on, let's dance," he said.

They stood up, cautiously put their arms around each other, and turned in circles a few times. Minnie Riperton was singing in high and desperate tones, and the song was far too slow.

"Really gay stuff, don't you think?" she said, and stopped. He was going to get angry again, but she pressed close to him and kissed his throat and his bare shoulders. Then she said, "Now the rose."

"Where?" he said.

"You know where."

"I'll have to moisten the towel again," he said with an odd smile. "It won't take long."

When he came back she was standing at the desk with her back to him. She had pulled her skirt up, her panties lay beside the laptop.

"The rose?" he said.

"The rose."

He pressed the tattoo firmly down with the wet towel, and as they waited he stroked her bare hips with one finger.

"Danny," she said.

"Yes?"

"Nothing."

Her voice was softer now.

"Danny, listen," she said. "I'm going straight home afterward, and you won't be angry, okay?"

"Okay."

He took the towel away and let go of her.

"Looks good," he said.

"It does?"

"It does."

"Describe it."

"Looks real. Looks like a genuine tattoo."

"I think I like it myself."

"I don't understand you," he said. "I mean, it's over. Or isn't it over? I thought it was over."

She turned and looked at him. She was holding her panties; he took them from her and threw them away somewhere.
Then he took her by the chin, a little too roughly, and kissed
her.

"You're getting on my nerves," she said.

"And you're getting on mine."

He tried to lead her to the bed, but she resisted and said,
"Come into the bathroom. I want to see what it looks like."

They went into the bathroom, she climbed up on the edge
of the tub, and, turning her head, looked at the rose on her
small, white behind in the mirror over the washbasin.

"Great," she said, laughing out loud.

"Do you really like it?" he said.

"Yes."

"Whose idea was this anyway?"

"Mine!"

"Are you sure?"

"Yes."

She laughed again.

He helped her down, and suddenly she had a brush in
her hand. Slowly, she brushed her long black hair, looking at
herself in the mirror.

He stood beside her and looked at her. She put the brush
down, and they looked into each other's eyes in the mirror at
the same time. Whenever she passed the brush through her
hair it crackled slightly.

"Or isn't it over?" he said.

Her eyes immediately filled with tears, and she said, "If I close them the tears will fall out."

"Close them, then," he said.

"No," she said, "it wouldn't be right, not here."

"Charles Trenet," he said, "I'll put Charles Trenet on, right?"

She nodded.

He went out of the bathroom, and a few moments later she heard "La Mer" playing in the apartment, quite loud. She waited for him to come back, looking at the butterfly on her breast in the mirror. She liked the butterfly, she liked this evening, and she liked being here. She smiled—but then something happened to her face, she slowly slid down onto the bathroom floor and closed her eyes. Tears rolled slowly out of the corners of her eyes, over her cheeks and down her throat.

The Suicide

It was two in the afternoon, the June sun was burning on his face, and he wanted a beer, and then another beer directly after it, and perhaps another later. He seldom used to drink beer, but recently nothing else would do. He would drink one or two glasses quickly, feel the warmth in his chest at once, and be glad of something without knowing what it was. And that wasn't even the best of it.

When the waiter came he had only to nod. The waiter nodded back and disappeared into the shadows behind the bar. Sami turned his face to the sun, and it was even hotter than a moment ago. The sun was everywhere. It shone on the white tables where people sat outside on the sidewalk and on the wide expanse of the sea beyond, which was blue as a mirror.

He was sitting by the window, and the window was open, but the sea wasn't a sea, it was Kastanienallee. However, in summer Kastanienallee *was* the sea. You just had to sit so that you didn't look past the heads and shoulders of the people sitting there and see the street. Most of them wore T-shirts and summer hats and sunglasses. The girls came in thin summer dresses, a woman would often wear just jeans and a bikini top, and they all kept looking at the sea as they talked. If you sat low enough on your bar stool you didn't see the cars driving down Kastanienallee. That made it even simpler to forget Kastanienallee and the buildings on the other side of the street. Only when a tram drove by did you know where you were. Then the tram was gone, and there was the sea outside again.

Lea was at the seaside too. She was standing at her hotel window in Tel Aviv, the window was tinted glass, and she looked down at the beach from high above. The gray waves moved slowly back and forth, the water was full of people whose heads bobbed about as they swam, and a little white boat was bobbing about too. Much farther out a tanker moved calmly by on the narrow strip of the horizon. Not a sound came into the room through the window, which was tightly closed.

"I'm ready," said a soft male voice behind her.

"Good," she said.

"Okay."

"Do we have to leave at once?" she asked.

"Not if you don't want to. We don't have to go at all if you'd rather not. And if you'd rather, then don't come with me, I'll go on my own."

"No."

"I'd be happy to go on my own."

I know, she thought. And then she thought: I must get into practice.

"Good," she said. "Go on your own and I'll stay here. Maybe I'll join you later. Would you like me to join you later?"

A tall, handsome, black-haired man in jeans and a white T-shirt placed himself behind her and stroked her hair. "Of course I'd like you to join me later."

She had brown hair with a few gray strands in it. It was her Iraqi grandmother's hair, and men always admired her hair first.

"Yes?" she said.

"Yes."

She didn't turn, but it cost her an effort not to. She waited.

"I'll be in the café," he said. "Anytime after twelve or so, that's what they said."

"Okay."

"See you soon," he said.

She went on waiting. Even when she heard him walking across the room, opening the door, stopping, looking for something in his pockets, and laughing quietly at himself for a moment, she went on waiting. But he didn't come back. He went out and closed the door behind him with a bang.

Perhaps he's playing a trick, she thought, and he closed the door with such a loud bang to make me think he'd gone. He's still in the room, and any moment now he'll put his arms around me and kiss me and maybe even push me down on the bed. She waited a little longer, then she turned around. The room was empty.

The third mouthful of the first beer was the best, thought Sami. The first mouthful burned your tongue, the second mouthful was still too cold, but everything was just right with the third. He drank the first mouthful, then the second and the third, and then he went on drinking fast and didn't put the glass down until it was half empty. He tried to remember what the other mouthfuls were like, maybe mouthful seven or mouthful twenty, but he couldn't. He did remember her last phone conversation with him, though.

"I know he'd do it," she had said before she went to Israel with Veit, on the pretext that they already had the tickets anyway. "I know he would, understand? He'd jump, he's often said so."

"Yes, he's often said so. It's only what he says," he had replied. Veit was lying, and Sami knew that she knew it, that Veit didn't mean it.

"You really think so?"

"Yes."

"What makes you so sure?"

"Because."

"No. No . . ."

"Yes. He doesn't want it to end, and he thinks a little blackmail wouldn't hurt."

"That would be so corny."

And it would be even cornier, thought Sami, if he really jumped. But then he'd be finally gone, you had to look at it that way too, and she certainly wouldn't miss him. In fact it was rather a pity that Veit was lying.

The second beer wasn't as good as the first. The third would taste good again. It would help him for two or three hours, and after that it would be as if he hadn't drunk anything at all, perhaps even worse. He'd drink it all the same. It was worthwhile being optimistic for two or three hours. Knowing for two or three hours that Lea loved him, loved him very much, just needed a few weeks, one or two months at the most, before she left Veit, whether he jumped or not, knowing all that helped him to hold out. After the third beer he wouldn't even think the trip to Israel was such a horrible idea.

I'm so horrible, Lea was thinking at almost the same moment. She was standing at the window again, looking down at the Café Orient. But Veit is horrible too, she thought. Sami's the only one who isn't horrible. Or no, Sami is horrible as well. He thinks he knows everything. I tell lie after lie, and he thinks he knows how things really are. That's the Jewish part of him, and I can hardly stand it. But of course he thinks I like it.

At last Veit came out on the white steps in front of the hotel.

Through the tinted glass of the window they looked gray. He stopped, put his blue Yankees cap on, and went slowly down the steps. Then came the sand—that too was gray through the hotel window—and Veit took off his sandals and crossed the beach to the café. He walked calmly and without haste, although the hot sand must be burning the soles of his feet.

Veit was always calm. He was calm when the food failed to arrive in a restaurant, when baggage didn't come off the plane at the end of a flight, when his father lay dying, when Lea told him about Sami to make him jealous. Of course a man like Veit would never think of suicide or threaten it. Usually he just smiled gently when there were any problems. And he had smiled last night when he told her that after Israel they ought not to see each other for a while. She wanted to sleep with him all the same, so they slept together, and he kept smiling in the same way. Only when he came did his expression briefly change.

Before Veit went into the café he stopped. He looked out at the sea for a long time, and his tall, attractive body still looked tall and attractive even from up here. Then an army helicopter flew over the beach, and Veit looked up at it. Lea retreated from the window in case he saw her, and then looked out again. Now Eli, Orit, and Dieter arrived too, along with two other people she didn't know. They went into the café together, and Ran, the man checking up on guests at the door, knew them all, nodded, and let them straight through. He watched them go in, then he waved to someone, Veit came back, they spoke briefly, and Ran looked up at the hotel as they talked. This time Lea didn't conceal herself.

When Sami got to his feet his legs didn't go with him. In fact all of him stayed behind on the stool, which was much too low: his back, his arms, his thoughts. He went uncertainly over to the bar, paid, and went out. Outside he leaned against the warm wall of the building and waited for his arms and legs in the sun, but they were in no hurry to join him.

The sea was gone. It was as gone as if it had never been there and would never be there again. Instead, a tram drove slowly and noisily around the corner. It came from Veteranenstrasse, another tram was coming the other way, and after they had both passed Sami decided to go back inside. He sat down by the window again, on his stool. His legs were still there, and so was the rest of him. The waiter was still there too, but Sami didn't want anything. He would never drink a beer again. He knew it was funny that he knew that, but he didn't know why he was so sure of it.

And then he did order another beer. He had never before drunk six beers one after another. But then, he had never before waited a year for a woman. He had never before gone a year without writing anything, a year without calling his parents, a year without seeing his son, a year hardly eating, a year without living. One more beer, a cold lager, and then never again.

And what was Lea thinking at that moment? I must practice. I must practice being without Veit, she was thinking, because he's going to leave me. She leaned her forehead against the warm windowpane and passed her hands over her small, dark belly, as she often did. She would like to go down to the Café Orient, but she wasn't going to do it. She wanted to sit beside him, and lean her head against his shoulder once or twice, and light two cigarettes and give him one. She wanted to watch him listening to the others in his pleasant, calm way as they laughed and talked in Hebrew and became hysterical, and only Veit was perfectly calm, so she was too, which meant more than anything to her. Well, that was over. Perhaps she could manage without him, but more probably not.

More and more people came into the café. The line grew longer and longer, and Ran kept waving more guests through without checking up on them. Ran was a nice guy, a simple soul but nice. Everyone who visited the café a few times made friends with him. He and Lea often used to joke together. He asked her in Hebrew, in front of Veit, when she'd finally go out with him. That German, he said, was no use to her. She said a Moroccan had even less to offer her than a German, and they both laughed. She laughed more than he did. It was only after a few days that Lea noticed how like Sami Ran looked. He was a kind of Moroccan parody of Sami, no hair, not much of a nose, lips rather too full, eyes much too clever. Since that occurred to her, she'd felt guilty when she saw him. She ought never to have told Sami that silly story about suicide threats, she'd made it up only to avoid making a decision. She thought of that when she saw Ran, so she didn't joke with him anymore.

There was suddenly something going on down there. Two of the men standing in line began pushing and then hitting each other. Some of the others in the line stepped to the left, others to the right, and the line briefly moved like a live snake winding back and forth. After a while the others separated the fighting men, order was restored, and it was as if nothing had happened.

I feel belligerent too, thought Lea. She imagined herself beating Veit on the chest and arms with her fists, and of course he didn't defend himself. He just smiled slightly, and that made her so wild that she hit him in the face, but he went on smiling. So she imagined picking up an ashtray from the table and smashing it into his forehead. Blood flowed over his forehead and his smiling lips, and Lea hit him again. He fell down, she kicked his silly, smiling face, and his head rocked back and forth. After a while she was exhausted, so she stopped, and she knelt over him and stroked his bleeding face. As she did so she thought, Maybe I ought to try it with Sami after all.

Lea opened her eyes and saw that she still had her forehead pressed to the windowpane. She raised her arms and pressed her hands to the glass as well. She was sticking to this large, gray, warm windowpane, she wanted to break free of it, but she couldn't. She looked down at the flat, ugly, concrete building of the Café Orient where Veit was now sitting without her, just as he would always be sitting somewhere without her in the future—and then she saw Ran running up and down in agitation, making strange gestures.

Ran took out his cell phone and called someone, and as he called he stood on tiptoe and tried to look over the heads of the guests into the café. Suddenly there was a stormy sound in the café, and for a few seconds everything down there was normal: the people standing in line, the gray, bleak concrete slabs paving the beach promenade, the shimmer of gray sand, the shimmer of the gray, half-naked bodies of the people on the beach, the gray shimmer of the sea. But then—and it was all as quiet as if someone had muted the sound on a TV set— Lea saw the flat, white roof of the café bursting apart, a huge, yellow jet of flame rising, she saw pieces of masonry, splinters of wood, and metal parts flying through the air, she saw the people outside the café being blown away like scraps of paper. At once there was another jet of flame and a pulsating black cloud, and through the closed window Lea heard a soft, distant explosion. She was stuck to the windowpane, she could make no sense of what she was seeing. Then she slowly slipped down past the pane, slid to the floor, and lay there with her eyes and her mouth wide open.

At the moment Veit died, Sami decided to have another beer after all. It was the best beer of the day. It was at the right temperature, and the little bubbles tickled his tongue and his throat pleasantly. He looked out the window, and the sea was back. So were his arms and his legs and his thoughts. At last he could go home, and he thought, That's funny, something's changed, but I don't know what.

Two Israelis
in Prague

Maybe yes, maybe no. Yes, yes. No, no. Yes, I like him telling me what he sees when he's kneeling behind me. No, I don't like it. I like it that he never takes off my bra. Nonsense, I hate it. I like being weaker than he is. No, I want to be stronger. And what about when he says you can go deeper in, it doesn't hurt me? That's really exciting. No, it's disgusting. I'm alone when he's with me, but I'm alone when he's not.

She carefully moved away his arm, which was lying on her hips, and got up. He went on sleeping, but he was sure to wake up soon.

She went to the bathroom, then she washed her hands, spending a long time on scrubbing her right forefinger with the nailbrush. After drying her hands she cut her fingernails and then washed her hands and that finger again. Then she went into the living room, sat down on the sofa and wondered what to do next. She had no idea. She didn't want to get dressed yet, but she didn't want to get back into bed with him either.

Yes, yes. No, no. Sometimes it went on for hours. They started, stopped for a while, sat down in the kitchen, drank water, and smoked. They lay down again, watched TV for a little while, talked, did it again. They didn't stop until she couldn't go on anymore, and she told him yes, all right, now. After that they talked a little longer, without any fire in their conversation. Next time the fire usually flared up again.

"Mali?"

"Yes?"

"What are you doing?"

"I'm in here."

She heard him get out of bed and go to the bathroom. His bare feet slapped on the floor. He put the seat up with a loud bang. Then he turned on the shower. The water fell against the side of the bathtub, there was rushing in the pipes, and it was as if he'd always been there. I could get used to those sounds. No, I couldn't.

She took the blue wool blanket off the armchair, wrapped herself in it and knelt down in front of the stereo system. She was looking for something quick, something to distract her mind. She took CD after CD off the pile and built them into a new pile beside the first. Then she put them all back again.

He turned off the shower, and she heard him singing quietly. Mostly he sang Israeli songs. Any moment now he'd come into the living room and dry himself in front of her. Three, two, one —

The bathroom door opened and his footsteps quickly approached. The floor shook slightly.

"What are you doing, Mali?"

"Looking for a CD."

"Shall we have another cigarette before I go?"

"Yes, let's."

He bent over her from behind and tried to kiss her ear. It was due to both of them that he didn't succeed. She moved back, he wasn't determined enough. A drop of water fell from his hair onto her bare shoulders. He wiped it away, and she pressed close to him. He held her tight, and suddenly she wanted him to stay.

"You could sleep here tonight," she said.

"What's the matter with you? *Ma kore i'tach?*"

"It'll be light by the time you get to Modřany."

"I like that."

"Anything you say."

She pressed close to him again, took his hand and kissed it. She kissed each of his fingers, and they smelled of soap and water. She thought of her forefinger and hoped it smelled just the same.

"Will you make some tea, Mali?"

"This late?"

"Very well, I'll get dressed."

He let go of her, and she heard him standing behind her for a little longer as he dried himself. Then he went barefoot into the bedroom. He was singing something again.

There was still a stack of CDs that she hadn't listened to for years. She went through them slowly, looking at each cover. Her old CDs from Israel were right at the bottom.

"Put Arik Einstein on!" he called from the bedroom.

I hate Arik Einstein. No, I don't hate him. Of course I hate him. If Mama hadn't always listened to his stupid "*Atzu Ratzu*" whenever she had a new boyfriend, maybe Arik Einstein wouldn't be any problem to me. Yes, he would, silly hippie music.

"Do you like Yehuda Poliker?" she asked softly.

"What did you say? I can't hear you."

"Shall I put Yehuda Poliker on?" she asked, her voice still low.

"No idea what you just said, but—yes. Yes, that would be nice. Yes, I could imagine that and more. Yes, I'll sleep here if you like."

"Do you know Yehuda Poliker's Polish CD?" she asked, her voice louder. "The one with the train?"

"Yes," he called. And then he added, "I see."

"Shall I play it?"

He didn't reply.

"All right, I will," she said softly.

Suddenly he was standing behind her again. She hadn't heard him coming.

"*Kol Israel chaverim.* Right, Mali?"

She turned to him and laughed. He laughed back. He wasn't very tall, he had red hair and freckles on his throat, and she was afraid of the moment when the door would close behind him and she would be all alone in Prague again.

He was already dressed, and there was a cigarette between his lips. "Where's the lighter?" he asked.

"In the kitchen."

"Whereabouts in the kitchen?"

"I'll come in a minute."

She was still kneeling in front of the stereo, wrapped in the blue blanket, holding the Yehuda Poliker CD. No, that wasn't music to distract your mind. It was slow, serious, Oriental, every note thrusting straight to the heart.

Yes, yes. No, no. I'm fine, I'm not so good. I want to listen to Yehuda Poliker now. No, I don't want to. It was really good to have done it again. Oh, God, how bad I feel!

She looked at the picture of the train passing by and the boy sitting on a grade-crossing barrier in front of it. Then she slowly folded back the cover and took out the CD. She read the titles—"Radio Ramallah," "Love Kills," "Flowers in the Wind"—and her nausea felt worse. When she turned the CD in her hands a little rainbow shimmered over the thousand near-invisible grooves.

"Mali, where's the damn lighter?"

"In the right-hand drawer."

"I've looked there."

"Then up on the dresser beside the ashtray."

"No, it isn't."

"Then I don't know either."

"Like some tea?"

"We've had tea already, right?"

"Not often enough, *chamuda.*"

She smiled. She put the CD into the player, but after a few bars the music stopped of its own accord. She took the CD out and found a mark on the little rainbow. Perhaps it could be removed, perhaps not. She licked her forefinger— and almost threw up. It didn't taste of soap and water, it still tasted of his ass.

"Found it."

"Start smoking quickly, please start smoking really quickly."

"What?"

"I didn't say anything."

She pressed play, and this time the CD played. She knelt in front of the boxes and trembled, and hoped he would never touch her again, never look in her eyes again, never speak to her again. She thought how nice it was to get up alone in the morning, sit alone in the Slavia in the middle of the morn- ing, walk home alone in the evening from the embassy along Nerudova Street.

Then she stood up and went into the kitchen and made tea. She drank tea with him, and smoked, and thought about what to wear to work tomorrow. When he left she kissed his cheeks. As soon as he was out of the place she closed the door behind him. She heard him quickly running downstairs, she heard the front door of the building opening and falling heavily back into the lock. She went into the bathroom and washed her hands thoroughly again.

Happy Ending
with Sticky Tape

It began with the bottle of vinegar that he absolutely had to take with him on his latest move. It took only a few movements, but they were as assured as if he'd done nothing else all his life. Sticky tape over the top of the bottle, turn the bottle slowly around, taking care that the sticky tape didn't slip. Finally take a small bite through it with his teeth, tear it quickly, and run his tongue along the smooth, sweetish-tasting side of the brown tape. After the vinegar bottle came the jam jars, not that it was really necessary with them, then the backgammon board and the drawers of his filing cabinet. Before the moving men rang the bell he also taped up the receivers of his phones, and while he was at it he took his girlfriend Annika's beloved teddy bear and, with a triumphant smile, turned it into a dark-brown mummy wrapped in packing tape. Then he immediately threw the mummy into the garbage in alarm.

Primo Tischmann, as he himself said, was not a practical man. But no sooner did he have a roll of sticky tape in his hands than he became a kind of god of sticky tape. There were no net curtains on his windows, only remnants of fabric from Karstadt's department store which he fixed to the window frames with his sticky tape. The pictures in his new apartment did not hang from hooks but were surrounded by artificial frames of packing tape. He used nothing to remove crumbs and dirt from the kitchen floor but the sticky side of packing tape. And as it was so practical, he stuck all his furniture to the floor one day, so that when visitors came and made a mess of everything, he had no difficulty in remembering which chair had stood where when he was tidying up after them.

For twenty-four years Tischmann had known nothing about his talent, or perhaps it ought to be called his inclination. Twenty-four long years from which sticky tape was absent, years in which to other people, those normal people who crossed his path, he was nothing but a reclusive character who wore elbow guards. But now he'd show them all! Tischmann was sitting in his office as he thought this, checking the same column of figures for the fifth or sixth time. What was he going to show them? he asked himself in some alarm. And how would he do it? Resigned, he shook his head. Then he looked at the time. And as he always looked at the time at just the right moment, it was exactly five. He turned off the computer, changed from his comfortable work shoes to his hard English walking shoes, and left the office. First he ran a wet comb through his hair in the bathroom and waved sadly to himself in the mirror.

That night, when his neighbors were already all asleep, Tischmann's doorbell rang. She looked neither as he had imagined her nor entirely different. She was simply dressed— gray trousers, some kind of silk blouse, small red earrings— and she spoke with an educated accent. The only hint of her profession was the way her lips closed and opened again slightly as she listened.

"Where?" she said, after he had given her the money.

"In the living room," he said. "Please, you go first."

She went in, sat down on the sofa and waited. For a while he watched her through the crack between the door and the door frame. She didn't look uneasy, but he knew just how she felt about him. They all felt the same way about him, although no one ever said anything. It was just that they always wanted to get away quickly. Would Monika want to get away quickly too? On the way to the kitchen he wondered if that was her real name. He took a new roll of tape out of the cupboard under the sink and went back to the living room. He sat down in the armchair and placed the roll on the table.

"What's your name?" he said.

"Monika."

"And your real name?"

"Claudia."

Obviously there were other people in the world who were at least as peculiar as he was.

"Do I do it to you or you to me?" she said impatiently.

"I . . . I'll do it to you."

"Then what?"

"I don't know," he said. He circled the roll of tape around his outstretched forefinger. Suddenly he said, "I don't think I thought this over enough. Please go now."

Flashback: Primo Tischmann, aged twelve, in sports class, the weekly handball game. Balls whistle around his ears like revolver shots, he feels like throwing himself to the ground and taking cover, but Dr. Kanurke, the sports and geography teacher, calls every few minutes, "Come on, come on, come on!" So little Primo stands in the way of the biggest of the opposite team and waits to see what happens. Nothing happens. They all stampede past him like a herd of buffalo, and Kanurke goes on shouting, "Come on, Primo, come on, come on!" Tischmann himself doesn't know why this is his most outstanding childhood memory.

On his way to the office the next morning Tischmann

thought of that Bulgarian who wrapped whole bridges, buildings, and trees in plastic film. The man was world-famous — and no one thought *he* was crazy. Monika certainly thought Tischmann was. At least, it was quite likely that she did. He knew for certain with Annika. She'd refused to come and see him anymore since he entered into his sticky-tape phase. How brave of her! Annika's face, glasses and all, was as lopsided as a Picasso painting, and before Tischmann she had never kept a boyfriend for very long.

At midday Tischmann called Annika. At first she wouldn't talk to him. She said he knew he wasn't to call her at the office, or indeed at all. Quarter of an hour later they were sitting opposite each other in Europa Espresso, saying nothing. Tischmann ate quickly and paid. As usual, he paid only for her meal, and later she would pay for his. They had agreed on this method at some point because she didn't want to be his guest all the time. And he didn't like them both paying just for themselves.

Over the next few days they met again more frequently. They almost never talked to each other, and sometimes Tischmann called Annika at home late in the evening, and they said nothing over the phone for minutes on end.

"We could stop seeing each other," said Tischmann the next week, after they had been sitting together in silence in Europa Espresso for half an hour again. Annika nodded. She took her glasses off her lopsided Picasso face, and now she looked like Munch's *The Scream*.

"We ought to have done more talking," she said. "Don't you think so?"

We ought to have done more with sticky tape, thought Tischmann. We ought to have tried it just once, to see what it's like doing it together. The next moment he jumped up in panic, horrified by his own crazy idea, and ran out of the bar as if running away from himself, never mind the separate paying. It's only a phase, it doesn't mean anything, it gives me a sense of security, he thought when he was back at his computer in the office. A little later all the toilet lids in the men's bathroom were stuck down with sticky tape, and so were the ashtrays in the waiting room and so was the emergency exit behind the elevators. When everyone had left in the evening Tischmann slipped into the boss's office and stuck sticky tape all around his desk. It would take a very sharp wallpaper knife to get it off again.

What a great vision: Primo Tischmann is king of the world and, in his own way, ensures that peace, wisdom, and justice prevail. Idiots have their mouths stuck closed, bad guys are stuck fast to their wives, warplanes can't take off anymore because they're stuck to the ground. Ugly pictures and ugly buildings disappear behind an impenetrable wall of sticky tape, meaningless party conference slogans and No Parking signs are covered with brown tape, and a little packing-tape treatment by Tischmann's packing-tape police makes it impossible ever to open books that no one ought to read. Later, much later, long after Tischmann has been toppled from power by the Scotch Tape Party and sent into exile, people begin remembering the days of his rule, they describe it as the golden age it never really was.

"Are you feeling more like it this evening?" said Monika when she was back in Tischmann's apartment one night.

"Yes," said Tischmann. "I hope so."

"Where?"

"Like last time."

She took the money and went into the living room. She sat down on the sofa and lit a cigarette. When she saw that her odd customer had now stuck sticky tape over all the windows and walls and even the screen of his TV set, she quickly put the money down on the coffee table and decided to get out of there at once.

"Please stay," said Tischmann, who once again had been watching her for some time through the crack between the door and the door frame. "Please save the world from me!"

Very early the next morning Annika was outside Tischmann's door. She couldn't ring the bell because it was stuck up, so she knocked. She wanted to see Tischmann before he went to the office, to tell him she accepted him the way he was. That day she was almost as beautiful as a Modigliani girl. She knocked softly and timidly at first, then harder and louder. But no one opened the door. Something must have happened, thought Annika, something terrible, I'd better call the police.

Then the door opened. The man suddenly standing there in front of Annika in the twilight of the corridor of the building looked like Tutankhamen risen from his tomb. He said, in Tischmann's voice, "It's a terrible strain being crazy." And then he said, "I think I'm okay again now."

A delicate carmine tint in the style of the early Impressionists covered Annika's cheeks. One leg crooked behind her, she leaned her upper body toward the mummy, and kissed it where she assumed Tischmann's mouth to be behind the thick, brown packing tape.

About the Author

Maxim Biller was born in 1960 in Prague. A critically acclaimed writer and columnist, he is the author of several short story collections and two novels, *Esra* and *Die Tochter (The Daughter)*. Biller's short stories have been published in the United States in the *New Yorker*. He lives in Berlin.